Going Home for

CHRISTMAS

34 Stories Set in the Christmas Season

Eric Foster Rhodes

❄

authorHOUSE®

AuthorHouse™
1663 Liberty Drive
Bloomington, IN 47403
www.authorhouse.com
Phone: 1-800-839-8640

This book is a work of fiction. People, places, events, and situations are the product of the author's imagination. Any resemblance to actual persons, living or dead, or historical events, is purely coincidental.

First published by AuthorHouse 10/5/2009

ISBN: 978-1-4490-2964-7 (sc)

Printed in the United States of America
Bloomington, Indiana

This book is printed on acid-free paper.

Acknowledgements

"Chickie's Gift" originally appeared
in *Cats* Magazine
"Mother Comes Home" originally appeared
in *The Rockford Review*
"Santa's Wrapping Paper" originally appeared
in the *St. Petersburg Times*

34 Stories Set in the Christmas Season

Introduction

O nce, on a long driving trip, I began to think about all of the many possibilities of people's experiences with the sole relating element being that the happenings would occur during the Christmas season. Thus, no one story would have to be tied directly to the religious holiday, or be related to any church or religious denomination. These would merely be interesting or happy or sad accounts of events in lives of people - sometimes adults, sometimes children - events which they experienced during what many of us think of as Christmas time.

So, as the miles sped by, I tried to imagine some of the many situations and locales and some of the limitless types and personalities of young adults, older people, children of varying ages, and to picture the complications and involvements that might arise. And sometimes, but not always, solutions to those complications.

I had finally outlined, in my head, then on paper when I stopped the car, thirty stories. Then, as I drove on, I thought of others I wished I had included. Then, finally, I decided to make the limit thirty-four. They were eventually written, sometimes rewritten, and here they are: thirty-four stories of the Christmas season.

The editors and publishers and I sincerely hope they will be stir memories, sometimes, and your imagination, sometimes, and that they will give you pleasure.

Going Home For Christmas

He was in the army hospital, he was ill, and Christmas was a few days away. Every time he let his mind turn to that, he experienced a deep empty feeling, different from the coughing and fever. It would be his first Christmas away from home.

To him, it seemed that everyone in the ward was coughing, great hacking coughs, even at night when they were blended with snores, contrapuntal sounds like tubas to the coughing horns. He thought he wouldn't sleep, but he did. Then awoke hot and with a raspy throat.

The nurses were kind, but brisk and impersonal. They made him take pills, and they took his temperature several times a day. He couldn't eat the food, but drank juice. Then it was only two days before Christmas, and the thought about home, only fifty miles away since he had been transferred back to this camp for advanced training. But, he told himself it might as well be a thousand miles.

When the nurse came this time, a doctor was with her. She took his temperature while the doctor listened to his chest.

"Well," said the nurse brightly, "temp is normal today for the second straight day."

The doctor looked at his throat, eyes, ears. "Umm, If you're normal tomorrow you might go back to the barracks."

The reclining patient grasped the doctor's sleeve. The doctor frowned, but didn't snatch his arm away. "What is it?" The doctor asked.

"Doctor," the patient said, urgently, "doctor, I only live fifty miles from here. There's a bus from camp." He paused, looking anxiously into the doctor's eyes. "Couldn't I go home for Christmas? Just for a day or two?"

The doctor looked at the nurse, then back to the patient. Suddenly feeling he had a chance, the patient added hopefully, "It'd be better for me than the barracks."

A slow smile crossed the doctor's face. "If I were only fifty miles from home, I'd want to be there." He took a pad from his pocket, began to write.

"Nurse," the doctor said, his tone lighter than before, "I'll have the hospital issue a two-day pass to this soldier. And here is the medication he should take with him." He handed the nurse a prescription. "If his temperature is normal tomorrow morning, we'll let him check out."

The nurse took the slip of paper, looked doubtful, then smiled hesitantly. "Yes, doctor."

The patient watched them move away. His heart was beating rapidly. He couldn't keep a smile off his face. Now, for the first time, he thought about the December weather.

Struggling up, putting on his robe and slippers, he moved toward a window. Weak, he thought. His legs were shaky, but he got to the window, held to the frame, and looked out.

Snow! Snow was falling thickly. Must have just started, he thought, because the ground was only lightly covered as yet, and no one coming through the ward had mentioned it. He shivered, watching the flakes fall through the grayness of the winter day.

Tottering back to the bed, surrounded by the intermittent coughing of the other soldiers, he thought of his mother and father. And of his girl friend. The thoughts again brought a smile to his lips, but then a flash of caution blinked across his mind.

Suppose the snow turns into a blizzard? Suppose it gets too deep and the buses won't run? He thought of the train line which had a station near the camp, and which went into his home city. Suppose it, too, could not run?

He didn't want to tell his parents or his girl that he was coming home, then not be able to make it. So he lay disconsolately in his bed, hoping for a successful trip from the hospital tomorrow. Tomorrow, Christmas eve.

During the night, he was awakened twice, to take medicine, to have his temperature taken, to the snores and coughs around him in the darkened room.

"Is it still snowing?" he asked the nurse, who was taking his pulse.

She nodded, made a note, then said, "Seems to have turned to sleet." She moved away into the dark.

At last it was morning, and he even had an appetite for the scrambled eggs and toast. "I'm going home today, nurse," he said, eagerness in his voice.

The morning nurse looked at him, frowning slightly. "Did the doctor say that?" He nodded emphatically. "Yes," he said, "a two-day pass."

Moving to the window, the nurse narrowed her eyes against the brightness outside. "Have you seen the snow? And sleet on top of it?"

His expression showed worry now. "It's not too deep, is it?"

She turned back to check his pulse. "It looks pretty icy and dangerous to me."

But the doctor signed the pass, and weak and shaky, the patient dressed in his uniform for the first time in a week.

"Check back on Christmas night," the doctor said. "We want to be sure you're all right."

The heavy army overcoat made him feel even less strong, but he walked carefully to the entrance. Did he have enough money for the bus and taxi fares, he wondered. Yes, he thought so – then he saw the road in front of the hospital.

Ice over snow. The storm was over, and early morning sunlight was dazzling with reflections from ice crystals. "Gosh, it must be cold," he said aloud. He studied the road. The ice had not been cracked by any vehicles' wheels as yet. Maybe it's too thick, he thought.

But just as he began to fear that the bus wouldn't come, there it was. Three or four other early passengers were on it. He had seen their faces before he began moving his feet cautiously over the ice to the open door of the bus. He made it without falling, and the heat inside the bus was a palpable wall, through which he pushed himself.

As soon as he was seated, the warmth made him sleepy, but he moved his face closer to the cold frosty glass of his window, watching the sparkly ice-covered snow move by.

Suddenly they were on a hill, descending, and he heard the driver say, "Oh, oh! Hold on tight, everybody!"

And he realized that the bus's brakes were useless on the downhill ice. The vehicle was sliding, first slowly, then faster, out of control. His heart began to thump as he watched in horror, the bus swerving across the road and back again.

At the bottom of the hill, the road curved away to the left. But the bus could not be turned out of its skid. It bumped sickeningly across a frozen ditch, then slid on across a field, then gradually, like a skater gliding on a rink, the rate of speed diminished, and at last the bus came to a delicate stoop, unharmed, poised daintily on the ice.

The driver looked around at the passengers, his face showing the remains of his panic, but his voice was calm. "Well, folks, we ain't going nowhere on this bus." He paused, studying the soldiers in their seats. "I guess you guys was all going off post on leave. Well," he pointed through the side window, "that there's the train station. It's about 100 yards across the field. Maybe they're going. It's either walk over there or walk back to your barracks."

The soldier from the hospital braced himself against the cold, and, climbing down from the bus, began taking tiny steps to balance himself on the ice.

"Good luck," the bus driver called. "This bus will probably be here when you get back."

Tiny step after tiny step, sliding shoes across the ice. The soldier was afraid to look up from his feet, afraid he would be appalled at how little progress he had made toward the train station. His breath came in short gasps, and a couple of times he was seized by wracking coughs.

But he was surprised to find himself, before he expected it, at the corner of the station building. As in the bus, when he entered the building, he felt physically assaulted by the heat. Yet it was welcome. He had begun to shiver.

The ticket agent told him the trains were running. "We had guys out with blowtorches and sand before dawn. You should get to the city okay."

And the train did come. he got a seat, and again watched icy drifts moving past his square porthole of vision. And they arrived in the city, an hour late but safe.

The bustle and battle for taxis was frantic. In his weakened condition, he could hardly compete, but at last the crowd thinned, and a civilian, a middle-aged man in a suit, got the next cab then turned to look at him in his heavy uniform coat.

"Here, soldier, you take this one. I'll get the next."

"Thank you, sir. I really appreciate it," the soldier said weakly, collapsing into the taxi seat.

The older man smiled at him, closing the door. "Well, you're doing your part for the country. Hope you enjoy the holiday."

The city's streets were full of slush, broken ice not yet slush, and many, many cars. But eventually the taxi arrived at the street address which was its destination.

The soldier paid, climbed out slowly, looking out at the front door of his parents' home - his home. A wreath with a red ribbon was on the door. He felt a wave of warmth, then was afraid it was fever.

The taxi moved off, and he inched his way carefully on the still icy porch steps. And then he knocked, and then there were his mother and father, eyes wide, concerned, delighted.

"Why didn't you call? Come in! I know you were sick. Are you better? You look a little weak. Sit down." His mother didn't wait for answers or responses. His father interjected his own questions and comments, smiling all the while.

But at last they fell silent, and he told them of his adventure. His mother said he needed hot soup, and went to make it. His father helped him out of his ice-and-slush covered shoes.

And then he reached for the phone, dialing his girl's number. His smile broadened when she answered. "Hi," he said, "It's me - I'm home for Christmas."

The Bicycle

She wanted the bicycle in the worst way. Two or three of her friends had shiny new girl's bikes, and it embarrassed her to ride that dumb old boy's bike that her cousin sometimes let her borrow. Especially now that the girls had their shiny new ones.

A girl of eleven with her own new bike would have real standing with her classmates, she told her mother and dad. And she had seen just the greatest one at the hardware store - dark red, almost maroon, with white trim. It was the neatest!

And it only costs $59, she told her mom and dad at breakfast. She was a little puzzled by the strange look which she saw pass between them. But she went on chattering about how Linda's bike was blue, and Ellie's was kind of a tannish gold color. Red would just be the coolest.

This conversation took place in November, great bike riding weather. But nothing happened. After a suitable period of time, she raised the issue again with her mother. "What do you think my chances are with dad on getting the bike?"

Her mother looked up from the dishes she was washing. "It's an awful lot of money, dear, I don't know if dad thinks he can do it right now."

She thought about pouting, but her mother's sad expression changed her mind. Instead, she looked out the window at the autumn leaves and said, "Maybe for Christmas, mom?" She paused. "I wouldn't really want anything else. You know, I could go without some other presents, if that would help get the bike." She looked again at her mother. "Gee, I really want it mom!"

Occasionally she would raise the subject again when both her parents were present, and she noted from time to time the strange pained looks which the seem to exchange. But she thought, maybe for Christmas anyway.

In mid-December an incident occurred which, at the time, seemed unrelated to any of her concerns. But one day her dad called her into his work room.

He said, "I just wanted to show you something. You know I like you to see things and know things."

She looked around at his tools, and said, "What is it, dad?"

He opened his wallet and pulled out five $20 bills, spreading them apart for her to see. They looked crisp and new.

"You don't often get to see $100 all together at one time," he told her. "I borrowed ahead on a piece of work I'm doing."

She looked at the money, her eyes wide. "Gosh dad. That's a lot." She didn't know what else to say, so she looked away.

"You can go back to your homework. I just wanted you to see that while I had it."

On Christmas morning, there was a shiny dark red bike - almost maroon - with white trim standing by the tree. When she came down from her room that morning, she squealed with delight, running to hug her parents.

Later in the morning, they walked with her, she pushing the bike, to the nearby park. While they watched, she climbed aboard and pedaled off as if born to it. As she turned in a wide circle, her parents applauded and laughed, and she laughed with them.

Years later, and more mature, she realized how difficult the times had been for her parents the year she coveted her bike. And she realized at last the connection between the borrowed $100 which her father had shown her and the bike which appeared on Christmas morning.

As the years had worn on, she grew to appreciate the sacrifices her parents had made. Gestures which, when made, were taken lightly or overlooked, now she thought back to with new insight.

She kept the bike for twenty years.

Christmas At The Sewer Works

Francie, reporter's notebook in hand, stood outside the entrance to the city's main sewage plant. An unmistakable odor hung in the air. "I must be crazy to be doing this," she told herself.

Then she shook her head. "No," she told herself, "it's my editor who's crazy. Or else he has a grudge against me. Why could he possibly think readers want to know what the sewer workers do at Christmas?"

She squared her shoulders. "But," she said aloud, "it's the job." She laughed, her young smooth features producing a dimple on each cheek. "Like, I imagine the sewer workers say, 'It's a dirty job, but somebody has to do it.'" She laughed again, and walked up to open the door to the office.

To her surprise, she found a neatly dressed young man, in clean shirt and slacks, neatly trimmed hair, neatly shaved face, sitting at a desk. The nameplate on the desk said, Bill Carver, Supervisor.

She advanced toward him, extending a business card. "I'm Francie McGuire? I called? You're Mr. Carver?"

He smiled. Rather handsome, she thought. He pointed to the nameplate. "Unless I'm here under false pretenses." He laughed.

She covered her embarrassment. "May I sit down? I hope I won't take too much of your time." So saying, she sat in the visitor chair.

She extracted a pencil from her purse and held it poised over her notebook. "My editor seems to think there's a human interest story about what sewage plant workers do at Christmas time."

He laughed again. "Most of them go home to their families and play with their kids and decorate their trees like everybody else. They're people."

Francie felt a flush creeping up her neck. This was not going at all well, even by comparison with what she had imagined. Finally she said, "I mean - I know they do that. But I get the idea that some of you have to work right through Christmas night and Christmas day and New Year's night and New Year's day. Is that true?"

He smiled and nodded, smoothing his hair with his left hand. Francie didn't see a ring. He pointed to a schedule on the wall.

"The city's sewer system is mechanized. There's lots of pumps and machinery needed to keep everything running - to keep the sewers flowing, so to speak." He looked at her with a kind of elfin glance, as if he wondered whether he should shock her with other terms relating to sewage. But he waited for her to respond.

She nodded. "So, is this right? At least some people have to be on duty? Do they - " She groped for the right term. "Do they actually do work, or are they kind of here in case something breaks or to check on things?"

She thought he was taking a devilish pleasure in her discomfiture. Smiling again, he said, "If you really think about it Ms. McGuire, fixing things that break is a kind of work. And even checking on things to see if they are running right is a kind of work." He paused. "Just like writing newspaper articles is a kind of work."

She felt the color rising into her cheeks. She felt she was being played with. But she said, "I see." She made a note. "How many people will work Christmas Eve? How many will work Christmas Day? And New Year's Eve? And New Year's Day?"

He leaned back into his chair and again referred to the chart on the wall. "Normally, throughout the system, we may have as many as fifty people working. But nights and holidays, we don't dig sewer trenches or make normal maintenance repairs. We do those during regular working days." He looked again at the chart, pointing to the day that represented December 24. "So on a normal night, or a holiday, we would have three or four people in this building. Somebody in charge. A maintenance engineer. A guy on call to go to any trouble spot. And a guy that rotates through the different sewer pumping areas to check them on a regular basis."

She made additional notes, and then looked up brightly. "And the other days?"

He smiled tolerantly. "The other days are the same. We have to have minimum people available at all times. We have to have them where they can identify any problem that comes up. Christmas Eve is no different from New Year's Eve. Christmas day is no different from New Year's day. We have a certain number of other people on call in case we have to have additional emergency workers. That's it. Big story, huh?"

Again she felt the color in her face. But she nodded and pretended to make additional notes. Wait till I get ahold of that editor, she thought.

Another question occurred to her, and she looked up from her notebook. "And do you have all these days off, because you're the top person?"

He smiled, looking into her eyes. "I could. I make my own schedule. But some of the men and some of the people downtown at city hall might think I was taking too many liberties and too many perks. And I would think so too. So I work my rotation, and my assistant works his."

She looked at him expectantly. "So," he continued, "I'm scheduled for Christmas Eve and New Year's Eve. My assistant is scheduled for Christmas day and New Year's day. That's his preference. He likes to be home with his family Christmas Eve and New Year's Eve It doesn't matter to me."

She tried to keep her voice steady. "You're not married?"

He sat back and grinned at her. Putting his hands behind his head and lacing his fingers together as he leaned back in the chair, he said, "I was born in Cleveland. I'm 29 years old. I have an engineering degree from Case Tech." His eyes twinkled. "I'm not married and I'm not committed. There might be a longer story about when and how I've been tentatively committed. But we won't go into that."

She sat looking at him, feeling flustered. She didn't know if she trusted what she would say. After a moment, she simply said, "I guess that's all I need for my article. You've been very cooperative. Thank you so much."

His position was still the same, leaning back in the chair. His eyes still twinkled. He said, "We have a little kind of an informal Christmas party here every Christmas Eve. The day workers stay over for a while after 5:00, and the first shift of night workers come in a little early. Some of the guys bring their wives. Some guys bring their girl friends." He looked at her again. We'll have refreshments, and each person brings a small anonymous gift. We trade those around."

She looked back at him. "Oh. Oh," she said.

"So," he said, looking into her eyes. "Would you like to come as my guest? I'll even donate an extra present for you."

She sat up straighter. "I can certainly very well bring my own anonymous gift. And I will." Again she felt flustered. She thought she had not responded as she had wished. "So thank you. I'll be pleased to do that. I'll be here."

He nodded and stood up extending his hand. She took it and felt a warm and friendly pressure. "At 5:00?" he asked.

She nodded, still holding his hand. "At 5:00. That's fine." She extracted her hand. Thank you again." She turned to leave.

Outside, the December day seemed not so drab. The odor hanging around the sewer plant seemed not so repugnant. Her editor seemed smarter than she had thought.

The Expedition

When Eddie and his parents had lived in a small village, he and his dad would go to a nearby farm the week before Christmas to cut a Christmas tree. They would pay the farmer and bring the tree home in the family car.

So, every year, as Eddie grew from four years old to nine, their home would be redolent of fresh cedar, sometimes pine, from late December into January.

After Eddie's family moved to a large city, because that's where the work was, they had to be satisfied for a couple of years with trees which had been cut a long time before December and far, far away - perhaps in Canada, or Michigan, or Maine.

These trees from city lots were not so green to begin with, and not so redolent of evergreen forests, and they never, never lasted past early January. Mother, father and Eddie each year studied their second-rate trees and reluctantly made the best of them. It was a bit discouraging when hanging glass ball would bring a pre-Christmas shower of dry needles. The floor had to be swept almost every day.

So, at age eleven, in their third year of the city, his dad looked up from his newspaper one December evening and said, "Eddie, why don't we drive out to the country Saturday and cut our own tree?"

Eddie smiled broadly. "Wow, dad! That'll be great. We can pick a really good fresh one. Can mom go, too?"

His mother, overhearing from the kitchen, said, "No, I think I'd better get the house cleaned up, so it'll be ready when you get back. You and dad have a good time."

When Saturday morning came, the first thing Eddie realized was that it was very cold. He first noticed this after jumping out of the warm covers, then, after putting on his robe and slippers, he went to the window, laced with ice, and peeked through at the thermometer mounted outside.

The red line stopped at 8 degrees Fahrenheit. It was 9:00 a.m. "Dad," he said, seeing his father enter the living room, "guess what the temperature is."

His dad laughed. "It was 7 when I looked. It's probably up to 8 or 9 by now." "Boy, we're going to be cold. I'll probably wear two sweaters under my coat." "Well," his dad said, "We'll have the heater on in the car. If we get good and warm, then we just want to get the car as close to the trees as we can."

Eddie's mother made sandwiches and put them in a paper bag with a few Christmas cookies. His dad started the car after some effort, then got the heater going. A few minutes later, they were off. It was 10:30 Saturday morning.

As Eddie's dad drove out of the city, Eddie said, "Good it's not snowing, hah, Dad? At least the sun is out."

They had been on a rural road only a short time when an ominous lump-lump, bump-bump came to their ear. The car began to list to the side. Eddie's dad wrestled with the wheel. "Feels like a flat, Dad. Is there room to get off the road?"

They managed to get the car onto the dead grass at the shoulder of the road, and climbed out. With the trunk opened. Eddie helped his dad lift out the spare tire. "Boy, oh boy, Dad. Good thing we've got gloves, huh?"

Even with gloves, changing the tire was very cold work. The lug nuts didn't want to turn with the grease so thickened by the freeze, and Eddie's dad had to stand on the wrench handle.

By the time they got back in the car, they were both shivering violently. "Well," said Eddie's dad. "We'd better find some place to get hot chocolate or something."

But they drove several miles - to the next tiny village - before they came to a store with a lunch counter. Hot chocolate reduced the chattering of their teeth. It was 1:30 when they left the store.

Another 50 miles and they were at the farm Eddie's dad had been aiming for. The stopped on the dirt road by the farmhouse and paid for a tree, then drove as close as possible to the field where there were trees available for cutting.

"Lucky we didn't forget our saw and hatchet, huh, Dad?" Eddie said bravely as the stepped across the field. It was 2:45.

They circled several trees, looking for symmetry, greenness, and ideal height. Most were too small, too large, or irregular in shape. Finally, Eddie's dad, said, "We're not going to find the right size. We're going to have to cut the top out of a large one."

So they selected what appeared to be a well-shaped top, and Eddie's dad began to saw through the trunk at about shoulder height. The saw wouldn't cut easily through the sap-filled wood. Eddie pulled on one side while his dad tried to saw through the widened cut.

Finally, the last inch of trunk snapped off, Eddie falling on the cold turf with tree on top of him. He laughed, rolling it off him. But he and his dad, momentarily warm from exertion, were chattering their teeth again as they dragged the tree toward the car. The time was 4:10.

Only a part of the tree would go into the trunk, and they had to tie the trunk lid to the tree limbs to hold the tree in and the trunk lid down. Eddie's dad climbed behind the steering wheel and started the car.

"We'll get some heat here in a few minutes." He looked at his watch.

The watch showed the time: 4:30.

"It's going to be dark soon, son," Eddie's dad said. "We need to get out on the main road, and we need to find a gas station."

Eddie leaned over to look at the gas gauge. It showed about one quarter full. "We can't get back without more gas, can we, Dad?"

His father shook his head. "No. If we hadn't had that flat, and if we hadn't had to stop for hot chocolate, and if we could have picked out a tree faster, we'd have had plenty of time to find gas." He looked at the gauge as they pulled away. "Now I'm afraid some of the stations out here will close."

The sun was already showing only an orange half-circle above the fields as the car headed for the paved road. By the time they were back on paving and headed for the nearest village, a reddish tinge showed at the horizon. Heavy shadows closed in on the landscape. It was 5:15.

Eddie and his dad peered past the headlights into total darkness, until at last a few house lights sparkled ahead. "Wasn't there a gas station here?" his dad asked.

"I think it was where the other road branched off," Eddie replied. Watching carefully, they at last saw the gas pumps. The pumps were dark. The station was dark. "Closed," Eddie said.

"Well, we'll just have to go on," his dad said. "It must be about 15 miles to the next village. The time was 5:40. The gas gauge showed an eighth of a tank.

"I wonder if the gauge shows what's really in the tank," Eddie said. "Hope it shows less, not more."

In the pitch dark, they rolled on toward the next populated place. After what seemed much more than 15 miles, they saw lighted windows and his dad flashed the signal, turning right.

Slowing to watch carefully, they at last saw the gas station they remembered. It was totally dark. "Everybody closes at dark," Eddie said, a tremor in his voice.

His dad pulled the car off the road, bringing it to a stop by the dark pumps. "Well, we're in a little trouble, son. We don't have enough gas to get to the next town. We're better off here then out in the woods or fields." He peered through the side window.

"What'll we do?" Eddie asked, trying to sound brave.

"Well," his dad said, "Maybe I can find somebody who'll let us in where it's warm. Let's start with that. Hope they don't think we're burglars."

Telling Eddie to wait in the car, his dad climbed out. Bitter cold flooded into the car in the brief moment before the door slammed shut. His dad's shadowy figure merged into the blackness in a moment.

Time seemed to creep like as thick molasses, as if time itself was slowed by the bitter cold. Eddie wondered if his dad was lost. His eyes became accustomed to the blackness, but he could see nothing moving.

Just as he was thinking he should get out to look he perceived movement in the darkness. He hoped it was his dad, then saw that it was, and that there was another figure as well.

In a miraculous moment, the gas pump light came on, and in their glow Eddie saw a man in a heavy machine turning the crank on one of the pumps.

Eddie's dad opened the car door a couple of inches. 'The people next door told me where the station owner lived. I walked down there, and he was kind enough to come out and let us get gas."

Eddie watched the man in the machine now begin to pump gas in to their car. In a few minutes he saw his dad pay the man, and then they shook hands. The man then came to Eddie's window and tapped on it.

Eddie quickly lowered the window a few inches. "Hi, young man. Looks like you got a good tree. Merry Christmas!"

"Merry Christmas!" Eddie called through the window as his dad started the car. Their lights picked out the black-topped road toward home.

Eddie twisted his body to get comfortable as hot air from the heater cut into the chill on the interior.

"We'll remember this tree, huh, Dad?" he said, trying to laugh, but still shivering. In his two sweaters under his overcoat, he finally began to feel warm.

Four Daughters
And A Son

Three days before Christmas, a stricken old lady fights desperately for life, writhing in her hospital bed.

In the corridor, carolers pause before each door, singing of peace on earth. In the sickroom, nurses monitor the agonies of a heroic struggle.

In the waiting room, four daughters and a son suffer silently, alternately staring at the floor and looking up to watch nurses hurry back and forth down the corridor.

"Why can't the carolers go away?" the daughter in the red sweater says petulantly. "Who needs that racket?"

"If mom can hear it, I'm sure she doesn't mind," the eldest, gray-haired daughter answers soothingly. "I know you're upset but mom won't be."

Red sweater shakes her head. "It gets on my nerves."

The son, lean and tanned from outdoor work, says, "Well, sis, we're really here for mom, aren't we? I guess we can stand to hear a Christmas carol."

"Silent night, holy night," the carolers sing, now further down the corridor.

"Do you think mom knows anything?" the youngest daughter asks. She looks anxiously from face to face. "She seemed unconscious when I looked at her."

The stylishly-dressed daughter answers. "I think she knew me. She squeezed my hand when I talked to her."

The daughter in the red sweater laughs disdainfully. "You always have to be better than anyone else. Why should she squeeze your hand? When was the last time you saw her before tonight?"

"Just one minute, smarty-pants," the stylish one says cuttingly. "What have *you* done for her lately?"

The son raises his hands, palms opened in front of him. "Cool it, gang. We're upset because mom is having a bad time and we can't help her."

The gray-haired daughter nods. "We're here, and that's all we can do now. Let's not bite each other's heads off."

Far down the hallway, the carolers are singing, ". . .The hopes and fears of all the years. . ."

The sounds slowly die away as the carolers move through the exit. The daughters and son watch the nurses move on silent feet in the harshly lit corridor.

Finally, red sweater says, "How are we going to pay for the funeral? None of us has that kind of money."

The youngest daughter leaps up from her chair. "For God's sake, she isn't even dead yet. So shut up!" After a pause, when the others give her stricken looks, she says, "And we'll find a way if the time comes. We'll find a way."

Again each person studies the floor, studies his or her hands, not making eye contact with the others.

After a long silence, the stylish one says, looking at her watch, "I have to go to work in the morning. I don't know how much longer I can stay."

Red sweater stares at her scornfully. "Oh, we know how important you are. What, have you already taken a couple of days off because your mother died?"

The son looks fiercely angry. "Knock it off!" He bites out each word. "Don't make me ashamed of you."

Another silence. "I'll sure miss her, I know that," says the eldest. Again the youngest is on her feet, eyes flashing. The eldest holds out her hands. "I know, I know. But I feel so helpless."

Finally a nurse walks toward them. They watch her silently. When she is in the waiting room, she says, "Well, her struggles are over. She's at peace now."

Tears spring to the eyes of two daughters; the son and the others fight them back with grim resolve. A doctor has followed the nurse into the room.

"We did all we could," he says, seeming to feel awkward with his platitude. Looking from anguished face to anguished face, he says, "I'm sorry." He retreats from their teary stares.

The nurse says, "If you want to look in on her, you may. We'll need someone to sign some papers. Then I suggest you go home. There's nothing more you can do tonight."

The daughters look at each other, then at the son. "Can you do it for us?" says the eldest daughter, her voice trembling.

The hospital corridors have fallen silent, empty, echoing to their steps as the grief-stricken family walks to the parking lot. No one speaks, no one touches. Each is wrapped in a winter coat and private thoughts.

In the frosty late-night air, their breaths puff out in wisps of steam. Clouds have partially obscured the moon.

"Have a nice night," the guard calls out. "Three days to Christmas."

The Christmas Card

An insurance man always congratulates himself when he gets through the door and can talk to the prospect in his or her house - usually hers.

Frail little Mrs. Minter had smiled at me, opened her door wider, and said, "Oh, yes, Mr. Walters. You're with Interstate General. Won't you come in?" She stepped aside for me to enter the dimly-lit living room.

You always think it's your skill and charm that gets you in. You don't like to admit that, once in a while, someone may just want to have a visitor. But we all know in our hearts that sometimes you'd get invited in even if you said you were a bill collector.

"Would you like some tea or coffee, Mr. Walters?" She had me seated on her threadbare sofa and was taking little bird steps toward her kitchen.

"Tea would be fine, Mrs. Minter, if it's not too much trouble. Thank you," I said.

"Oh, no. No trouble. The water's hot. It'll just take me a minute or two." She was already in the kitchen.

My prospect card told me that Mrs. Minter was a widow, seventy-eight, and that she had one of our less expensive Medicare supplement plans which would pay some of her excess hospital costs.

While sounds of clinking china came from the small kitchen, I looked around the sparsely-furnished room. Two chairs with sagging upholstery, two small end tables, a coffee table with a lace doily, a small bookcase topped by a vase with dried flowers, and a 13-inch TV on a stand. On the wall, one framed flower print, and a framed photo of what must be some family members.

"Sugar, Mr. Walters?" her small high voice called.

"No, thank you. I drink it plain," I called back.

On the TV set, a single Christmas card stood, catching my eye with its bright red poinsettia leaf design. I got up from the low-slung sofa, drawn to the card by a sort of suspected recognition.

I picked up the card, looking inside. There, in imitation engraving, the message said, "Best Wishes for the Holiday Season. Interstate General Insurance Company."

As I set the card back in place, Mrs. Minter said, "Here you are." She set a cup and saucer on the coffee table. "I'll just get mine." Carrying her own cup, she returned in her small-step pace to sit in one of the upholstered chairs.

"Thank you very much," I said, sinking back into the sofa.

She sipped her tea, then set her cup on the end table. "I saw you looking at my Christmas card. It was very thoughtful of your company to send that out."

I sipped my tea, and made myself smile. "Well, you're a valuable client, Mrs. Minter."

She took her cup up again. "What did you come to talk about, Mr. Walters? I hope my policy is paid up."

I nodded. "Oh, yes. I just wanted to check on how things are going - whether you've been well. If you've had any medical claims?"

She had a frail little smile "I've been well. Of course, my arthritis. But nothing to put me out of commission."

"Good. Good." I opened my notebook. "Now, Mrs. Minter, as I recall, you were going to consider changing to our more comprehensive medical plan - so that more of your hospital bills would be taken care of when an accident or illness occurs." The language was straight from the agent's training manual.

She looked at me plaintively. "I so wish I could help you, Mr. Walters. I know you have a family, and you need to sell insurance. I always help when I can, but my money is so limited just now."

I tried not to look shocked. She wanted to buy for *me*, but she couldn't. "It's really something for your family, Mrs. Minter. So your children don't have to use their savings when you're ill."

Her head shake was a small, dainty movement. "I'm afraid my children died, Mr. Walters. My boy was killed in Vietnam. And Nancy was in an automobile accident. It's a blessing they had not married."

I sat very uncomfortably still. "What of your other relatives, Mrs. Minter?"

She placed her cup carefully on the end table. "I'm all alone, now, Mr. Walters. My sister passed away last year."

A silence ensued. "Maybe if I can make a few economies, I'll be able to help you later, Mr. Walters."

I shook myself, trying for a smile. "It's I who want to help you by improving your insurance protection, Mrs. Minter." I paused. "But I guess I've intruded long enough for today."

She rose as I did and extended her tiny hand. "It's always a pleasure, Mr. Walters. Thank you for coming." As I turned to go, my eyes swept across the poinsettia leaves of the lone Christmas card.

When I entered the office, my manager looked up. "I don't see any applications in your hand, Bill. You hiding 'em in your notebook?"

I shook my head dismally. "Two not at home, two not interested, three thinking it over, one with no money. Pretty slow day, Fred."

Fred slammed his hand on the desk. "Not interested means you didn't sell yourself. Thinking it over means you didn't push for a close. No money means you bought an excuse. You're never going to get ahead if you let them get away that easy."

I sat down. It was as if he hadn't spoken. "Fred, would you believe that this little old lady, Mrs. Minter, has one Christmas card in her house the week before Christmas?" He looked at me. "And it's ours. Interstate General. The kind the home office sent out."

Fred nodded. "Yeah. At first I thought just agents got them. But my wife got one as a policy holder."

I stared at my shoes. "There in that threadbare house, living all alone, her kids and her husband dead, she has one Christmas card. And it's ours."

Fred said, "So you got in, but you couldn't sell her, huh? Even with *our* Christmas card in her house?"

"Fred, she *apologized* to me for not being able to help *me* out. Said maybe she could make some economies later."

The manager looked at his desk pad. "Well, don't waste any more time on her, then. Minter, eh? Just hope she renews what she has. Get to work on something more promising."

I looked at Fred, who continued staring at his blotter. Finally I stood up. "Yeah, I guess I'll make some more calls this afternoon." I looked at the nameplate on Fred's desk. "Frederick Cooper, District Manager." Frederick Cooper, Scrooge and Simon Legree combined, I thought, and walked away.

The winter sun was near the horizon, casting a chill, reddish glow over the lawns and sidewalks as I turned my car into the street where Mrs. Minter lived. The afternoon had been a series of rejections and not-at-homes. The days before Christmas were unusually bad for selling insurance.

Finally, I had decided to call it a day, but I made one stop before finding myself on this street. Very few cars on this block, I thought. Lots of these people don't drive.

So it was with surprise that I saw a Crown Victoria which appeared to be parked in front of Mrs. Minter's house. A shock of recognition washed over me as the car began to pull away. It was Fred Cooper's car.

Shock became anger. "That bastard ran out here to try to steal *my* client. Try to twist a little old lady's arm to buy when she can't afford it. Damn!"

I grabbed my package and trotted up the steps to her porch. Wondering what I would say, I pushed the bell button, hearing the chimes inside.

When the door opened, Mrs. Minter's eyes widened in her delicate face.

"Oh, Mr. Walters! What a day for surprises! Do you know that nice Mr. Cooper was just here. He says he works with you, and that he's helping you distribute fruit cakes to your customers. And he brought me one. Wasn't that really nice of him?" She paused for breath.

I fumbled awkwardly with my package. Finally I managed a sheepish smile. "Yes, I guess he and I got our lists mixed up."

I held out the package. "I was just dropping by with your fruit cake. But I see he beat me to it."

Mrs. Minter laughed in her silvery voice and threw up her hands. "Oh, gracious, Mr. Walters. Please take that to someone who needs it. I can never finish even one. But thank you so very much."

I lowered the package, still with a weak smile on my face. Her eyes were sparkling. "And please come back when you can. It's always nice to see you." She paused, then her eyes widened. "Oh! I almost forgot."

She stepped away from the door, then returned quickly with a square envelope. "You can do me a favor and take this back with you for you and Mr. Cooper. It'll save me a stamp," she said in lighthearted voice. "And merry Christmas to you and your family, Mr. Walters."

As I retreated to the car, the fruit cake package felt like lead. I placed it on the passenger seat, then sat quietly, ignition key in my hand. Finally, I looked at the envelope Mrs. Minter had handed me. It was addressed in fine, spidery writing, to Interstate General Insurance Company.

I opened it and found a Christmas card showing a snowy small-town street scene. The message on the inside said, "At Christmas time, our thoughts turn fondly to our friends. Merry Christmas." And it was signed in the spidery script, "Lillian Minter."

I laid the card on top of the fruit cake package. Finally I started the car and pulled out into the reddish sunset glow. Window panes flashed fiery red reflections as I passed them.

I laughed softly. "Old Fred," I said. "Old Fred." And the farther I drove, the better I felt. After a while, I was laughing unrestrainedly. The driver of a passing car looked at me quizzically.

"Old Fred," I said again, and turned the car toward home. The sun was almost set. Christmas lights sparkled in darkening doorways.

Santa's Wrapping Paper

One of my early discoveries about Christmas was that Santa's gifts came wrapped in stiff brown paper, fastened with brown paper tape.

Presents from aunts and uncles, grandmothers and others all were enclosed in bright green or red paper printed with holly, sleighs, bells and things. And silk ribbons were tied with bows.

At about age seven I became aware of the unmistakable similarity between Santa's wrappings and those used by my father in his photo studio, in front of our home, where he wrapped framed photographs for delivery to the customer. The final moment of truth came on Christmas Eve, about nine p.m., when I strode unannounced into his workroom, and found the object of my letter to Santa, a tool box filled with tools, being wrapped in stiff brown paper by my father.

"Don't come in here when I'm working," he said, trying to look stern, but the damage was done. I knew - not just suspected - who Santa really was.

Not only were Santa's presents wrapped on Christmas Eve, but it was the practice in our town during those years for much of the Christmas gift shopping to be done on Christmas Eve. It was a short but intense shopping season.

The year following the tool box, I made it known during that magic period of early December, when toys appeared in greater quantities in the Main Street stores, that a shiny, gold-painted trombone was the object of my admiration. When my father and I were at the drug store soda fountain for a soft drink, I took his hand and led him across the store to the glittering toy department.

"Look at this, dad! Isn't that really neat?" I pointed to the trombone, making sure that his eyes followed my finger to focus on the coveted object.

"What about this camera?" He was always trying to interest me in photography. "That should be a good one for a boy your size."

"I shrugged, trying to be polite. "It looks nice," I said diffidently. Then, in a brighter voice, "but I never saw a trombone quite like that!"

Looking back, I think my use of the toy drum I received at age six may have given my dad pause.

But every day, as Christmas drew nearer, I visited the store, checked to be sure the golden trombone still rested on the display shelf. And occasionally I would find a reason to refer to it in conversation with my parents.

Eventually - in those days it seemed an eternity - Christmas Eve arrived. And sometime around mid-afternoon, I made one of my spot-checking forays into the drug store. Imagine the hollow feeling in my stomach, and the skipped beat of my heart, when I turned the corner of aisle to face the shelf where the trombone had rested - and it was gone!

That empty, forlorn segment of the shelf space evoked a look of misery - a realization of missed opportunity, of anticipated paradise lost. Nothing left on the other shelves seemed half as attractive as the missing instrument.

When I dragged myself into the house, my father looked at me for a moment, then said, "You feeling all right?"

I tried to pretend I was not devastated, but I just couldn't do it. "That trombone I liked is gone. Somebody bought it."

"Is that right?" he said. "Let's go make sure."

"No, it's gone. No use looking," I said miserably.

"Oh," my father said. "Well, I'm sure there are other things that are nice toys for boys your age."

At supper, as I slowly stirred my tomato soup staring into the bowl, my thoughts were on the child's camera I was sure was to be my lot from Santa Claus. And I tried hard to think I would like it.

That night, I walked in the dark street with my mother. Holding her hand, I admired with her the decorated houses, and paused to listen to carolers. And later, I put out my milk and cookies for Santa. And even though my father didn't drink milk, the glass was always empty the next morning.

When my eyes popped open with the first gray of dawn, I slid quietly out of bed, the feet in my sleeping suit protecting my toes from the cold floor. Creeping into the dim living room, I let my eyes adjust to the half darkness.

There under the tree were various brightly wrapped aunt and uncle and grandmother presents.

And there, near the front, was an elongated package in stiff brown wrapping paper. One end was enlarged in a bell shape. I knew in a moment of keen perception - I knew that it was my trombone. My father had shopped earlier than usual, I thought, my smile broadening to a grin from ear to ear. And who needs Santa Claus with a father like mine - a father with love in his heart and lots of brown wrapping paper.

The Matchstick Set

Herbie had seen it in the toy section at the drugstore. By comparison to other toys around it, it was small. It was, in fact, the size of a large matchbox, the kind that holds kitchen matches.

But it tantalized him and tickled his imagination like no tricycle, no basketball, no large set of building blocks, no cowboy hat could do. It was small. It was different. He wanted it. Badly.

What it was, the label on the box said, was a matchstick construction set. "A matchstick construction set," he said to himself, mouthing the words. In his mind, he saw it as an erector set or a tinkertoy set made very, very small.

And the smallness intrigued him, appealed to his imagination, made him want it more than if it had been large or even very large.

So he spoke to his father. Insisted on bringing his father to the drugstore and showing him the matchbox. To say the least, it did not seem to appeal to his father's imagination.

"Why in the world would you want a little cheap thing like that?" His father said with disdain. "Look at all these good things. You have a real tinkertoy set. Anything you build with this, even if it worked, would be so small and weak it would just fall down and break."

Herbie looked up at him. "But it's so teeny, Dad, don't you see? It's so teeny." He touched the box reverently, rubbing his fingertips lightly over its edges. "Nobody else will have anything like that."

His father laughed. "I believe that. I don't see why anybody else would want one." He took Herbie's hand. "Come on, son. Let's get an ice cream cone." So Herbie saw no hope from the avenue of his father. And being age nine and sophisticated, he saw no hope from Santa Claus either. And he knew that, in the world of buying things, the only way to his mother was through his father.

Things looked glum indeed on the matchstick construction set front. But Herbie was not ready to concede that the matchstick game was lost.

Herbie got an allowance. It was fifty cents a week at that point. This usually disappeared quickly on ice cream sodas or candy bars, but this week it hadn't disappeared yet, since the week had just started. And, miraculously, he had a quarter from last week, and he had some unknown number of coins in a piggy bank.

So, in the privacy and seclusion of his room, he removed the cork from the bottom of the ceramic pig and shook out the coins onto the carpet so they would not make a loud enough noise to attract his mother's attention. There was ninety-five cents in the piggy bank.

Herbie did quick math in his head, with the help of his fingers. "Ninety-five and twenty-five is - a dollar twenty. And fifty cents is a dollar seventy."

His dad had helped him buy a present for his mom, and his mom had helped him buy a present for his dad, so there was no problem there. This money was his free and clear. And the matchbox construction set was priced at a dollar forty-nine. So he was home free.

Except for one thing. He thought his father would be very critical of his spending his money on something which his father thought was a waste of money. And he thought his mother wouldn't be too thrilled either.

So he lay back on the rug and schemed. He thought of buying it and hiding it. But that seemed too sneaky, plus the fact that he wouldn't be able to play with it, for fear of getting caught. He thought of giving it to one of his friends, and then going to his friend's house to play with it every day. But he couldn't rely on his friends not to break it or not to want to play with something else when he came instead of the matchstick construction set.

"Be just like them to want to play cards or checkers or some dumb thing like that," he murmured to himself, picturing his friends.

At last he settled on what he hoped was the right idea. He gathered up the money - a dollar forty-nine - took an extra ten cents in case there was tax or something, and put the rest back in the piggy bank. No ice cream sodas this week. But Christmas was coming.

On Christmas morning after he had been to the living room with his parents and opened gifts and watched his mother and dad open gifts, Herbie said, "I thought I heard something at the front door." He ran down the hall, opened the front door, closed it again and came back. When he entered the living room he was holding a small box wrapped in plain brown paper.

"Funny I didn't hear anyone at the door Herbie," his mother said. "What's that you've got there?"

Herbie held the box close to his eyes, pretending to study the inscription on the paper. "Somebody must have dropped it off I guess, Mom. I guess it's for me." He held out the box for his mother and dad to see. "Some of my friends don't spell very good. Look how they spelled Herbie. H-U-R-B-Y. Ain't that funny?"

His father was studying the shape of the box. "Yes. That's funny."

His mother said, "I wonder what it is?"

"Yes," his father said. "I wonder what it is too." There was something unusually quiet about the way his father spoke.

Herbie unwrapped the box and, dropping the paper at his feet, held the contents in his hands. He showed it to his mother. "Look Mom. It's a matchstick construction set. It's just like that one I was looking at at the drugstore."

"Yes," his father said in the same quiet voice. "It is just like the one at the drugstore."

His mother looked with interest at the box. "Wasn't there a name on it or a tag, Herbie? Who sent it to you I wonder?"

"Yes," said his father. "I wonder too."

Herbie went through the motions of picking up the wrapping paper and studying it again. "No name on it, Mom. It must be an anonymous admirer!"

"Yes," said his father. "Anonymous."

So that's how Herbie got his matchstick construction set. And why he had to forego ice cream sodas during the week before Christmas.

But somehow, somehow, he never seemed to get the degree of pleasure or the high level of satisfaction which he had envisioned when his eyes had first lighted on the matchstick construction set on the shelf in the toy department at the drugstore. Somehow the few things he tried to do following the instructions never seemed to work quite right, and somehow he felt a little funny whenever he thought about playing with it. So, soon it lay in his toy box, and was covered with other lesser-used playthings of boyhood.

The Change Purse

Amy wanted to buy her mother a Christmas present. At age 8, it was hard for her to picture the real value of things, so she had gone from shop to shop, studying carefully what was available and at what price.

It was the time of the great depression - the mid-thirties in America. Amy's father had shown her the lines of men waiting to be hired for $1 a day. Many of them didn't make it. Amy's father was proud to be an independent shop owner. But some days nobody came, and some days he traded his goods for meat from a hunter or vegetables from a farmer, because most people had no money, or very little.

Amy and her mother and father lived behind their shop. Rent for the shop and living quarters combined was paid to the bank at a rate of $27 a month. Some months, the $27 was very hard to acquire. Amy knew this, but her parents tried their best to shield her from the worst impact of the times. Somehow meals were always there, and clothing to wear to school.

Last Christmas, Amy had asked her mother why Santa Claus brought presents for Amy but not for mother and dad. Her mother had told her that Santa Claus was for children, and not for grown-ups.

"But," Amy said, a small frowned her face, "how will you get presents?"

Her mother had smiled. "When you get bigger, Amy darling, you may want to buy momma and daddy a present. But you're not big enough yet."

Now it was December a year later. Amy had worked hard on a scheme to raise money.

The scheme was this: she had asked her father if she could do errands for him in connection with his shop. If she did, could he pay her? Her father had looked at her for what seemed a long time.

Finally he said, "If you make deliveries for me, Amy, when I need it, I'll pay you a nickel for each one. How's that?"

Amy laughed and clapped her hands. "Just what I need, daddy. Thank you. Do you have a delivery for me to make now?"

Her father looked at her again and then around his shop. "No one has anything to be delivered right now, love. But maybe this afternoon. Check with me then. Meanwhile you can play."

Amy had come back at 3:00. Her father said, "Well Amy, I need you to go to the post office and see if any packages have come for me. When you come back, I'll give you a nickel."

Amy had run off to the post office and asked the clerk whom she knew if her father had any packages. The clerk had looked around behind the counter, then come back and said, "No Amy. Not today."

And Amy had run back, reported to her father, and her father was ready with a nickel to place in her hand. "Be careful not to lose it," he said, looking serious. "Keep it in a safe place."

So Amy had run an errand every day. On a couple of occasions, she actually took something to someone. The other times, she was checking at the post office to see if something had come in. Each day, she added a nickel to her savings. So, by the end of the week before Christmas, she had twenty-five cents.

Then began the scouting of shops and stores to see what was available and what was the price. She quickly learned that, even in those depressed times, most things cost more than a quarter. This discouraged her, but she thought there must be something and she would find it sooner or later.

She was especially attracted to Miss Alice's ladies shop. She knew of course that something like a dress was out of the question. But her eyes would stray to the glass display cases where purses and gloves and bracelets and jeweled combs and other smaller things seemed to beckon her. Sometimes she could read the price tag on an item, and knew it was much too expensive. Other times there did not seem to be price tags, and she would ask Miss Alice. Always, the price was far beyond her means.

Two days before Christmas, she decided at the drug store to buy her father a hunting magazine for ten cents. She knew her father liked to hunt, and she thought he probably would not buy such a magazine for himself. She carried it into the house under her sweater, and hid it in her room until she could wrap it.

But that still left the problem of her mother. And now she had only fifteen cents left. Still she scouted from shop to shop and store to store and kept her eyes darting to everything which might be something her mother would like.

And now it was the day before Christmas. She had seen things in the ten cent store which could be bought for the sum she still had available, but it seemed to Amy that they were not worthy of her mother. Small mirrors, plain combs, plain handkerchiefs. It seemed to Amy that, for her mother, she should have something more special.

And so again she was drawn to Miss Alice's ladies shop. And again she dawdled before the glass cases, looking at the things she had looked at before. Again, Miss Alice watched her and waited for her questions. But questions were slow to come, because she had already priced almost everything in the cases.

Suddenly Amy noticed an item which she had not seen before. Lying on the velvet display shelf in the glass case, next to jeweled combs and near fine leather gloves, was a handsome leather change purse. True, it was small, as change purses are, but it had a gold or a gold-colored clasp, and the leather looked fine. The more she stared at it the more she thought, "Wouldn't that be nice for mama."

At last, she looked up, her eyes searching for Miss Alice. With real trepidation and a hollow feeling in her stomach, she braved the question. "Miss Alice. This change purse."

Miss Alice left her clerk with whom she had been conversing and moved closer to the counter. "Yes Amy? What was your question?"

"This change purse here, Miss Alice." Amy drew a breath. "What would be the price for it?"

Miss Alice looked at the purse then looked at Amy. "Well, Miss Amy. Would you be thinking of it for your mother?"

Amy nodded solemnly. Miss Alice smiled. "That would be a very nice gift for your mother. You have really good taste." She continued to look at Amy. "How much were you thinking of spending?"

Amy looked downcast. "I bought my daddy a hunting magazine, Miss Alice. And now I only have fifteen cents left."

Miss Alice's face became wreathed in a smile. "Why, isn't that the strangest thing!" She pointed at the change purse. "We had just decided today to mark that change purse down to fifteen cents, since no one had bought it yet. Imagine that!"

Amy could not believe her good fortune. But quickly, she reached into the pocket of her dress and extracted three nickels, laying them on the top of the glass case. "Oh, yes, Miss Alice!" She pushed the nickels toward the shop's proprietor. "I think it's just right for my mother. It sure is lucky that I came in now before somebody else got a chance to buy it." She was smiling broadly. "Please wrap it in tissue paper and I will take it right now."

Miss Alice reached into the case and lifted out the purse. From a shelf behind her, she pulled a sheet of tissue paper and enclosed the soft leather purse in it, then handed it to Amy.

"Merry Christmas, Amy. And I know your mother will have a Merry Christmas too."

"Thank you, Miss Alice," Amy said, and went running from the store.

The store owner stood watching Amy until her small body disappeared from view. Still she stood by the glass case. Her clerk walked up from the rear of the shop.

"Alice," the other lady said, "I saw you pay a dollar to the leather goods salesman for that purse. I saw you do it this morning. There hasn't been any time to mark that down. And you wouldn't take a loss on it anyway."

Miss Alice smiled, still looking towards the front door. "In almost any circumstance, I wouldn't. You're right. But sometimes there's a special circumstance."

She turned to look at her assistant. Her eyes were sparkling. "So," she said, "Merry Christmas to us, too!"

The Long-Term Tree

Elwood thought it was the best tree he had ever decorated. In fact, it was the first he had ever done single handedly.

In early years, he had first hesitantly hung a ball or two or an icicle or two under his mother's supervision. As he grew to six, then seven, then eight he assumed a greater share of the responsibility. At nine and ten he wanted to do the whole thing, but his mother had to help him out when he faltered.

But now, at eleven, he had done the whole thing without anyone else touching it. Its cedar boughs rose almost to the ceiling, its trunk reposed in a bucket, braced with bricks, and swaths of cotton batting wrapped the bucket and spread out as imitation snow around on the surrounding floor.

Every possible branch was fastened with glittering tinfoil icicles, and from every possible hanging point multi-colored glass balls and specially shaped ornaments depended. A family heirloom angel, made of blown glass and artfully tinted, topped the tree.

His mother admired Elwood's artistry when it was done. Standing hands on hips, she surveyed the corner of the living room now filled with cedar and glitter. "You did a wonderful job, Elwood."

"Thanks, Mom. It sure was a lot of work."

His mother nodded. "Yes, every year I feel that it is so much work to have to take it down again in a few days."

Elwood turned to look into his mother's eyes. "We always leave it up till New Year's, don't we, Mom?"

"Yes, I guess we usually do," she replied.

Elwood stared at the tree. "I wish we could keep it up until my birthday," he said wistfully.

"Your birthday? Good heavens, Elwood, we can't keep it up until February!"

Elwood spread his hands, "Well, Mom. You see it's in a bucket full of water. That's why I put it in a bucket, so it would stay fresh. If we keep it watered, I bet we can keep it till February."

His mother laughed, "What would people think of us having a Christmas tree in our living room after the first of the year? Nobody does that. It would just be too embarrassing."

Elwood walked around in front of the tree looking at it from every angle, thinking. 'The other kids would think it was neat to have it stay up longer."

When his mother did not reply, Elwood continued to stare at the tree. Suddenly he looked up, his eyes shining. "I know! After New Year's we can move it to my room! What do you think about that?"

His mother laughed again. "I think that's the nuttiest idea I have ever heard. Imagine having a Christmas tree in your room after the first of the year! I would just be so embarrassed."

"But don't you see," Elwood said in his most persuasive tones, "it will be in my room, and nobody has to know about it. When your ladies club comes in, they sit in the living room or they have refreshments in the dining room. And we will just keep my room door closed! Nobody will know a thing."

Elwood's mother looked at him, mixed emotions showing on her face. Finally she said, "Elwood dear, you know your father and I love you. We let you do lots of things. I don't think you want to do this. I think you will get over it."

Elwood still stared at his work of art which sparkling with reflected light. "Well Mom. Let's leave it here for now, we'll see."

Christmas came with its usual merriment and social activities with family and friends. Visitors came and went, gifts were put away and wrapping paper disposed of and the days moved on toward the new year. Still the tree stood in its corner.

On New Year's day, Elwood's mother said to him, "Well, we've kept the tree up as long as we can. I know it's harder to have to take the decorations down then it was to put them up, but I'll help you Elwood. Let's get started."

"Oh, no, Mom! You know what my plan is! You've got to let me do it. It won't hurt anything. Like I said, nobody will have to see it but me. It will be so neat to keep it up till my birthday."

His mother looked at him again. "Even if I let you do such a nutty thing, the tree is too hard to move. We'll knock decorations off and it will bump through the doorway and who knows what!"

But, after much pleading and reluctant assistance from Elwood's father and only a few balls and tinsel knocked to the floor and only a little water spilled, the tree took up its new residence in the corner of Elwood's room. He turned it carefully to have its best side out, replaced the few fallen ornaments, and replenished the water supply in the bucket.

"Oh, boy, Mom! This is really neat. Thanks to you and Dad for being such swell parents!"

Elwood's mother and father stood in the doorway, sheepish expressions on their faces. His father said, "Sometimes I don't know what gets into us." With a last look at the tree before turning away, he said, "Just be sure you keep it watered, son."

So the days of January slid by. The tree, despite all watering, grew drier and drier. A gradual collection of needles grew thicker on the white cotton below the tree, and on the floor beyond the cotton.

The showering of needles was accelerated and made more critical by visits of the English setter Teddie to the room. Usually Elwood was glad to have the company of the dog whenever it wanted to visit his room. But, somehow, Teddie's wagging tail always managed to impact the tree and send another shower of needles flying. In a desperate effort to preserve what were left of the needles, Elwood took to keeping his door closed against Teddie's incursions.

The arrival of February signaled two things to Elwood. First, he had accomplished his goal of keeping the tree. But second, now he had to undress it and dispose of it, whereas, if he had followed his mother's original wish, it would have been done a month ago and his burden of responsibility for the tree would have disappeared into dim memory.

His mother came into the room carrying boxes. "These are the boxes that the ornaments go in, Elwood. I'll help you, but we've got to get this done." She stood near the tree and looked at the fallen needles. "Good heavens, what a mess!"

So Elwood and his mother removed the decorations, stowed them away for another year, and then stood looking at the naked tree. His mother said, "I can't believe that even with that water bucket it got so dry."

Elwood said, "Wouldn't it be neat to burn it! You know that incinerator place out behind the stores where they burn things? I could take it there and set it up and have a real tree fire!"

His mother looked at him with raised eyebrows. "Well, you have to take it someplace to dispose of it. And that incinerator is as good as any place, I guess. But you're not supposed to burn things there. Besides, it's dangerous."

Elwood drew himself up to his full height. "Mom, I'm eleven years old. I brought this tree in and I can take it out and I know how to stand it up in the incinerator and nothing's going to happen."

Finally his mother said, "Well, get it out of here before your father comes back, so he doesn't have to do it. Try not to make any more mess then you have to. I'll be sweeping up and vacuuming for a long time in here after you've gone." She looked carefully at Elwood. "If there's a fire in the incinerator be very careful not to get too close to it. If there's not, just throw the tree in and come home."

Many more needles fell away as Elwood dragged the tree through the back of the house, down the back porch steps and across the backyard to the alley. Down the alley and around the corner was the open area where merchants disposed of used packing material and other refuse in a screened-in incinerator enclosure.

When Elwood arrived at the corner of the incinerator, he was disappointed to see that there was no fire burning. As he was about to hoist the tree over the fence, he thought, "Wouldn't it be neat to make it stand up and burn like it was a tree in the forest?" He looked around to find some way to stand the tree up, but the ground was frozen so hard that there wasn't a way to make an impression in it, let alone create a hole in which to place a tree trunk. Any attempt to lean it against the fence left it at an awkward angle or the tree slid over and fell down.

His eyes searching the area, Elwood finally focused on the brick wall which was the rear of a novelty store. "I bet I could stand it against that wall and it would do just fine. And bricks don't burn," he told himself.

When the tree was propped against the brick wall, he admired its perpendicular aspect.

"Boy I bet it would burn good there. Too bad I don't have matches."

When he wandered back to the area of the incinerator, he saw that there was still smoke rising from a heap of burned material. Poking at it with a stick, he lifted a charred piece of wood, and sparks flew out. With the added oxygen supplied by the raising of the charred ember, a new burst of flame shot out.

"Oh boy! Now all I have to do is find a piece of paper or a little stick that will catch on fire."

He found a small sliver of wood and inserted its tip into the new flames he had fanned. In a short while the end of the sliver was glowing red. Quickly he ran back to the tree leaning against the bricks, and touched the red stick to a branch. Smoke rose a moment and then suddenly the branch burst into flame.

Elwood jumped back as the very dry cedar skeleton went up in flames with a whooshing roar.

"Wow!" Elwood was astonished by the power of the flames.

It seemed only a moment or two before men and women were rushing out of doors near the end of the brick wall. They had terrified looks on their faces. "My God!" Mr. Willett, the store owner, shouted. "The whole place will burn down!"

Elwood was horrified. "But it's bricks!" he called lamely.

Mr. Willett grabbed a long stick and knocked the flaming tree away from the wall. "The heat is so high inside that I'm afraid everything will burst into flame in the store-room!" He looked at Elwood. "Don't you know bricks can get hotter than anything and they take forever to cool down? What kind of a nut are you? What was your stupid idea?"

Elwood was hovering at the point of bursting into uncontrollable tears. He knew he couldn't speak, or tears would follow instantly. So he swallowed hard, his eyes brimming, and just looked back in anguish.

At that moment, his father rounded the corner and took in the scene at a glance. "Get a hose, Bob," he said to Mr. Willett. "We'll spray it and cool it down. Quick!"

Mr. Willett ran back inside, and came rushing back with a hose which was part of his stock of merchandise. Elwood's father quickly hooked it to a spigot connection and turned the water on.

"Stand back!" He shouted. "This is going to make some kind of steam!"

As Elwood watched, his father began to spray water on the wall. As predicted, a great wave of steam was immediately produced. Everyone jumped back, and Elwood's father seemed to be lost in a cloud of steam.

Minutes went by before the steam diminished and the water had had enough cooling effect to simply splash back and run down the wall. Finally, Elwood's father turned the spigot and dropped the hose to the ground.

"Well Bob," his father said to Mr. Willett. "Let's look inside and see if anything is damaged in there."

Gradually everyone filtered inside the variety store, and, except for a little smoke and vestiges of steam, things appeared normal.

"Well," said Mr. Willett. "It looks like we were lucky. I guess you saved us, Fred," he said to Elwood's dad. "I don't know what got into the boy."

Elwood's father turned to look at his son. "Whatever it was, Bob, I have a feeling it's not going to get into him again." He turned back to the store owner, apologizing for their unfortunate experience. Then turning back to Elwood, he said, "Let's go home."

They walked in silence until they were near their back porch. "Do I have to tell you what an awful, stupid thing that was?" His father asked, looking into Elwood's eyes. Elwood shook his head miserably. "I heard you tell Mom that people learn by doing, Dad. So like you say, I guess I learned never to do that again."

As they were climbing the porch steps, Elwood looked back the way they had come. "But I guess that's one Christmas tree we'll never forget, huh, Dad?"

Three Wise Men - One A Girl

Because of an acute shortage of boys and an abundance of girls, one of the three wise men was a girl.

From the points of view of Ronald and Henry, known in their circle of ten-year-olds as Ronnie and Hank, many of the programs of the Sunday school were less than satisfactory because of this imbalance of boys and girls. To have to involve girls in your activities when you are ten is often excruciatingly embarrassing. Not that Jenny Sue wasn't reasonably okay as a girl. But still, she was a girl. So, how awful to have to include her as a wise man in their Christmas pageant.

"Now, boys," Mr. Edwards, the Sunday school director told them, "We're going to have a real good pageant here. But we have to have one of the boys be Joseph. And girls weren't innkeepers in those days, as far as I know. So that's what we've got Freddy tapped for."

Ronnie looked around at the gathered pageant designees. "Couldn't Hank and me be shepherds?"

Mr. Edwards looked at Ronnie with a touch of sadness. "There's shepherds and there's angels. To my way of thinking, angels are girls. And shepherds are boys. We've cut way down on the number of shepherds, but we have to have a couple."

He looked at Ronnie and Hank. "That leaves two boys and there are three wise men. Jenny Sue will do a good job." He smiled briefly at her, standing next to Ronnie. "So here are the scripts with your parts to speak. How about going over there in the corner and practicing?"

Ronnie cast a sidelong glance at Jenny Sue, all skinny and spindly, but with shiny black hair hanging down her back almost to her waist. She gave a quick smile and said in her girl voice, "Well, I guess we are stuck with it. I'll do my best. Come on, guys, let's start rehearsing."

She began to move toward the corner of the Sunday school auditorium, and, after a brief hesitation, Ronnie and Hank followed, carrying their pages of pageant action and dialogue.

As they stood together, reading the papers Mr. Edwards had given them, a puzzled frown crossed Hank's face. "I know what gold is, all right. And I kind of guess that frankincense is some kind of perfume, like incense." He looked up at the others. "But what the heck is myrrh?"

Jenny Sue looked perplexed, and then shrugged her shoulders. "Should we ask Mr. Edwards?"

Ronnie shook his head vigorously. "Heck no." He looked back toward where Mr. Edwards was directing Mary, Joseph and the innkeeper. "Whenever we ask him anything, he always says ask the minister, anyway. We should be smart enough to figure out what myrrh is."

Hank nodded, his eyes sparkling. "Sure. It must be a combination of something. It must be a word made up from the things that make myrrh." He looked slyly at Jenny Sue. "Let's think about it a minute."

After a brief silence, Hank said, "It must be mouse fur." They looked at him, eyes wide. "See," he continued, "M for mouse, and URR for fur. M-URR. Murr."

The three of them burst into uncontrollable laughter, after the manner of ten-year-olds. So devastating was their mirth that they quickly fell to the floor and rolled about, still laughing uproariously. Mr. Edwards, distracted from directing Mary and Joseph, looked at them angrily.

"What on earth can be wrong over there?" He started toward the corner. "I don't know what gets into you kids. We can't have this kind of thing if we're going to have a serious pageant on Christmas Eve."

Gradually, Ronnie, Hank, and Jenny Sue controlled their laughter, and slowly gasped into silence. "Now," said Mr. Edwards, "come over here. We're going to set up the manger scene and we'll walk you through your parts."

But that day, and each rehearsal thereafter, when Hank would say, "I bring my gift of myrrh," the three wise men - one a girl - would fall in helpless laughter to the floor of the stage. Nothing Mr. Edwards could do or say would be able to forestall this appalling outcome.

Finally, it was the day before Christmas Eve. It was the dress rehearsal. Ronnie and Hank cast sidelong glances at Jenny Sue, whose black hair had now disappeared beneath a jeweled turban, similar to the ones the two boys wore. Somehow, that metamorphosis, plus her wholehearted and helpless entry into their ten-year-old laughter, made Jenny Sue seem not too bad.

Mr. Edwards signaled to the three when it was their turn to climb to the stage. "Please," he said, "let's try to do it right. Tomorrow is the pageant." He looked at them dubiously. "Tomorrow."

Nevertheless, berobed as they were, bejeweled as they were, beturbaned as they were, when Hank uttered the fateful words, "I bring my gift of myrrh," the three exploded in helpless laughter, their minds picturing mouse fur.

Mr. Edwards was furious. He stamped his foot on the stairs leading to the stage.

He shouted "If you can't do it right, we won't have a pageant." He stomped his foot again. "If you can't do it right, there'll be no wise men. Do this tomorrow and you will embarrass your parents to death, not to mention everyone else." His flashing eyes sought to lock with theirs. "Your names will be mud."

Pulling themselves together, the three looked sheepishly at their director. "Let us try it one more time, Mr. Edwards," Hank said. "I think it's kind of my fault. If I can keep control, I think Ronnie and Jenny Sue can, too. Please?"

Mr. Edwards looked dubious, stood hesitantly for a moment, then nodded. "Okay. Now or never. Do or die. Let's try it."

And miraculously, the three wise men - one a girl - did their parts without blemish and stood beaming proudly when it was through. Mr. Edwards beamed also, his face showing a succession of emotions: surprise, relief, pleasure, pride.

"Okay," he said. "Good. Just like that tomorrow. Now let's go home and rest."

So the evening of the pageant came. It was Christmas Eve. Parents of the performers, relatives of the performers, friends of the performers, the minister and other church members gathered for the event. The hall was filled.

And the pageant proceeded smoothly. Mary, Joseph and the innkeeper played their roles to perfection. The shepherds were suitably solemn. The angels were airily angelic in their diaphanous garb.

When the wise men - one a girl - arrived bearing gifts, they were splendid and eyecatching. When they delivered their lines and their gifts, every word was perfect. Mr. Edwards, holding his breath at the side of the stage, let out a great sigh.

Ronnie, Hank and Jenny Sue had choked down their mirth when Hank offered his gift of myrrh. Laboriously, strenuously maintaining straight faces, they turned to exit from the presence of the holy child. As they started their journey back to the East, Jenny Sue stepped on Hank's trailing robe.

Hank, thrown off balance by the sudden jerk of his garment, stumbled over the top step leading from the stage. Jenny Sue fell forward, and Ronnie gaped in bewilderment. It was as if the flood gates were loosened. The dam had burst, and the pent-up mirth poured forth in gales of hysterical laughter as the three wise men - one a girl - lay partly on the stage, partly on the stairs, helplessly and hopelessly out of control.

For many in the audience that night, viewing the incomprehensible collapse of decorum, there was great bemusement. For the parents of the three, there was helpless humiliation. Mr. Edwards vowed that it was the last pageant he would ever direct.

Later, Ronnie's mother, waiting in the vestibule for her son to change from his costume, encountered the minister. "Oh, Reverend," she said in a quivering voice, "I'm so embarrassed for Ronnie. I don't know what to say."

The minister smiled sympathetically. Looking into her eyes, he said, "But, they are *children*." He spread his hands. "They are still *forming*."

When Ronnie, Hank and Jenny Sue, now attired in normal ten-year-old clothes, walked home through the night with their parents, there were long periods of silence. But the stars made twinkling sparkles on the snow. And tomorrow would be Christmas.

Christmas Alone

The old man opened his eyes to see morning sunlight streaming in through the window. He sat up slowly, creakily, and tried to focus on the room around him.

Feeling for his glasses on the nightstand, his fingers encountered them and he attached them to his ears and rested them on his nose. "Now, Mr. Mayberry," he said aloud to himself, "I think we'll see a little better with those glasses on." He looked around the room again. "Where's your robe, Mr. Mayberry?"

He found it at the end of the bed, slipped into it and into his bedroom slippers, and went down the hall to the rooming house bathroom. When he returned and had closed his door, he stood with his back to it, eyes staring out from his lined and shrunken face. "Well, Mr. Mayberry, what shall we do today?"

He walked to the closet, opened the door and looked at the few garments hanging there "Well, I think we'll get dressed. What do you say about that, Mr. Mayberry?"

Slowly, laboriously, he found and put on clothes, a shirt, not too soiled, a threadbare suit not too wrinkled, and finally a necktie not too spotted, which he carefully tied. "Mr. Mayberry never goes out without his necktie. People comment on that. It would be a shame to disappoint." Dressed in suit and tie, he now slowly made his bed. As he finished straightening the covers, he looked up at a dusty framed diploma on the wall.

"Need to do a little dusting around here, Mr. Mayberry. Now where did I put that duster?"

In the drawer of the small desk in the corner of the room, he found a well-used feather duster. Stretching to reach the diploma frame, he whisked the feathers across it.

"Yes sir. Richard Mayberry, Class of - " He stared for a moment at the diploma through the dusty glass. "Class of 60 years ago," he said very slowly. "Can you imagine that, Mr. Mayberry? Sixty years ago." He turned to look back around the room. Bed, wicker rocking chair, small desk with straight chair, table with small television, bookcase with perhaps a hundred books. Worn carpet on the floor.

"Probably should take a refresher course or two one of these days, Mr. Mayberry," he laughed. "Yes sir. Probably just about time for a refresher course or two."

Taking a worn grey topcoat from the closet, he went to the door, removing the key from the inside of the lock, stepping into the hall, closing the door and locking it. He put the key in his pocket and started down the stairs of the rooming house.

At the bottom of the stairs, he encountered Mrs. Oliver, another elderly tenant. "Good morning, Mr. Mayberry! And where are you off to?"

To himself, he thought, "You're a nosy woman." Aloud, he said, "Just thought I'd step down to the store for a couple of things. Nice morning."

A look of surprise flickered across Mrs. Oliver's face. "Why, the stores won't be open, Mr. Mayberry. It's Christmas morning. Don't you know the stores close on Christmas?"

His eyes were unwavering as he looked at her. He felt a small flutter of surprise, but tried not to show it. "Of course. It's Christmas. What I had meant to say, Mrs. Oliver, was that I was going down to the newsstand and pick up a copy of the newspaper." He continued to look at her. "Merry Christmas, Mrs. Oliver."

Her face still retained a partial remnant of dismay. "Merry Christmas to you, Mr. Mayberry."

He turned back toward the stairs. "And I just thought of something I need to do before I go out. So please excuse me." And he climbed slowly back to the second floor.

Unlocking his door again and stepping inside, he went to the closet. "Well, Mr. Mayberry," he said to himself. "It's Christmas. So, there is something that we must do."

Rummaging in one of the boxes at the back of the closet, he pulled out a Christmas wreath, its ribbon somewhat the worse for wear. "Here we are, Mr. Mayberry. We'll just hang this in the window as is our annual custom." He moved to the lone window and, holding a string loop attached to the wreath, he felt along the top of the window frame. "Ah yes. Here's our trusty nail. And here is our trusty loop. And the twain shall meet and the wreath shall hang."

When he returned to the lower level, Mrs. Oliver was not to be seen. He breathed a sigh of relief, and continued out the main door and onto the sidewalk. Turning toward the corner where the newspaper box was located, he began moving in shuffling steps.

"Well, we won't go to the store, Mr. Mayberry. Because it's Christmas Day. Strange how that slips up on one. Somehow I had quite lost track of the flow of days in this December." As he shuffled on, he tipped his hat to a lady walking her dog. "Merry Christmas, ma'am!"

Nearing the newspaper box, he said aloud, "So, Mr. Mayberry, we won't buy anything special. We'll just assume our regular routine. I believe we still have a can of tuna or two in the closet. And a little tuna and crackers will make a tasty repast."

He placed a coin in the slot of the newspaper box, opened the door and extracted a copy of the Christmas edition. He could tell it was the Christmas edition because there was holly printed across the top of page one. "Very festive. Very festive."

Another lady was passing him as he folded the newspaper to tuck it under his arm. She had a paper bag in each of her arms and the bags were overflowing with wrapped Christmas gifts.

As she passed him and he turned to follow, one of the packages slid from its precarious perch on the top of its bag, and fell to the sidewalk behind her.

"Madam! Madam!" he called. The lady slowed and turned her head.

Laboriously, he stooped to retrieve the package, then slowly straighten himself again. "I believe this package fell from the top of your sack. Permit me to restore it to you."

The lady smiled. To himself Mr. Mayberry thought, "Why she's not old for this neighborhood. She's a young woman. Probably sixty."

Aloud, he said, "I trust nothing was damaged when it fell. Allow me to restore it to the top of your bag there, and perhaps I can make it a bit more secure."

Her smile was broader. "Well, you certainly must have the spirit of Christmas, sir. I don't know if I would have even noticed that the package fell. And with my arms full like this, I don't know how I would have picked it up. Thank you so much."

As she started away, she hesitated, and then turned to look back where he was still standing. "You've added to my Christmas spirit, I know that." She turned again and continued walking.

Mr. Mayberry refolded his paper and again carefully tucked it under his arm. Watching the lady recede into the distance, he said aloud, "And you to mine, madam. You have added to my Christmas spirit."

He began his return trip to the rooming house, saying, "Yes, Mr. Mayberry. A little tuna and crackers, I believe."

Buying Everything

The people who lived two doors up the street - up the hillside - from me had the same size row house that I did. And they had two children, while my wife and I had one.

It was a few weeks before Christmas when I finally began to be aware of the enormous number of packages which were being transported in, day in and day out, by the lady and her husband. I began to wonder where they would keep them all, and I thought surely that most of them would be outgoing gifts which would leave the house again before Christmas.

I remarked about this to my wife. She said, "No, I've talked to her. Those are all things for their kids."

"I can't believe it," I said. "Do you realize how many packages and boxes have been going in that house?"

She nodded. "Yes. I was in there. You can't get into their family room downstairs. It's full."

I shook my head in disbelief. "What do their kids think about that? They are surely old enough to know what is going on. Aren't they like seven and nine?"

"Yes. That's what they are. And, according to her, they think it's super. Christmas is a super time."

I laughed. "Well, I hope our little girl doesn't get the idea that you have to fill your family room with gifts for it to be a super Christmas. How can they afford it?"

"Apparently they both work overtime the month before Christmas - maybe a couple of months. I guess they think it's worth it. I haven't seen the stuff they get, but I hope they're things that are good for the kids."

In fact, I had seen only the tip of the iceberg. Because I wasn't always watching, and because I wasn't always home, I must have missed a lot of the carryings in during the days of December. The reason I know this is because of what happened the day after Christmas.

The day after Christmas was a normal pickup day for the trash man. When I took my garbage can out, I looked up the street and I could only see as far as two houses. The view of the rest of the street was totally blocked by the enormous mountain of cardboard cartons, remnants of boxes and crates, and sacks of trash, much of it Christmas wrapping paper. The heap totally blocked the sidewalk, took up two parking spaces, and much of the small front lawn.

When the garbageman came, I heard loud voices and went out to see what the trouble was. The garbagemen were arguing with the man two doors up the street.

"You're only allowed two cans or the equivalent of two cans," one of the garbage guys was saying in an aggravated tone. "You couldn't stuff this stuff in twenty cans."

"Well," said the man up the street, "what am I supposed to do? This is our trash."

The garbageman looked around in disgust, finally said, "You've got two choices. I'll take the equivalent of two cans, and you got to leave the rest, or else I'll radio in for another truck and you will have to pay extra. That's your choices." He looked challengingly at the man.

The two stared at each other for what seemed a long time. Finally the man shrugged and said, "Call the truck. We've got to get the street cleared off here."

So that's how the trash mountain dilemma was resolved. Later that day I was walking up the street with my little daughter and I encountered the trash mountain man just getting out of his car. I spoke to him, and after additional pleasantry, I said, "I saw all that to-do with the garbageman today. Lucky they were able to get another truck."

He frowned. "Cost me a bundle. When people make trash, it seems to me the garbage people should take it away, not give you a hard time."

I smiled at him. "My wife says you and your wife really got a lot of Christmas stuff for your kids. She said you filled the family room with it."

He smiled. "Yes," he said, a note of pride in his voice. "We like to do things right for the kids. If they want a trampoline, we get it for them. If they want a Punch and Judy stage, we get it for them."

I looked at him for a moment. "How long have you lived here?"

He rolled his eyes, concentrating. "I guess nearly three years."

I looked at his house. "Aren't you gonna fill the place up pretty soon at the rate you're going? None of my business," I said quickly, "but I live in the house two doors down and they are the same size. I know you have limited room."

He laughed. "Well," he said. "You know, people have to live life the way they see it. We get a hell of a good time out of giving stuff to our kids." He paused. Then he looked back again toward his house.

In a voice that seemed filled with speculation, he added, "I guess maybe in a year or two we'll have to move to a bigger house."

And they did.

The Electric Train Set

Betty, in spite of being a girl, had expressed strong interest in an electric train set. Kenny had echoed her desire and leaped with enthusiasm when the idea was set forth by his sister. Betty was six and Kenny was five.

"I don't know," said their dad to their mother. "I couldn't have imagined Betty wanting a train set. We sure can't get two of them. And Kenny probably will be devastated if she gets it and he doesn't. What do you think we should do?"

His wife shrugged. "Every year, the decisions seem to get harder. I know we can't afford two sets, even if it was sensible otherwise."

They looked at each other speculatively. "What if – " They both started to say at the same time, then laughed.

"You first," the mother said.

Her husband laughed again. "All right. What if we get a train set and we tell them Santa Claus wanted it to be for both of them and it was to test how good they could be about sharing?"

His wife laughed again. "You're really asking for it, you know that?" The father smiled. "Why not make life interesting?"

"You mean more interesting."

So they hugged each other and kissed each other and looked ahead to the next chapter in the adventures of Betty and Kenny.

And when Christmas morning arrived, there were gaily wrapped gifts from mom and gaily wrapped gifts from dad and there were gaily wrapped gifts from Santa. One of the larger, heavier gifts from Santa turned out to be, when the paper was stripped off, an electric train set. Betty and Kenny whooped together in glee.

"Now, children," their mother said. "Let me read what Santa has written on his card." She picked up the paper which had been cast aside by the children, found the card, and said, "Now listen. Santa says this gift is for both of you."

Kenny looked at Betty and Betty looked at Kenny. Their mother continued reading, "You were both good children and you both wanted this train set. I want you to show me - that's Santa talking - that you know how to share and play together with the same toy. Merry Christmas!"

The father looked at Betty and Kenny, smiling, "So that's what Santa said, kids. I hope you enjoy it and I want you to show me and mommy that you know how to share and play together, just like Santa says."

The children were studying the package, which was colorfully inscribed with representations of the train, cars and tracks inside. "Help me open it up, Kenny," Betty said.

The kids fell upon the box and soon had it opened. Other gifts were temporarily forgotten. Mother and dad were temporarily forgotten, too, and stood bemused on the sidelines watching their children lost in awe and delight.

Piece by piece, the train cars came out and stood on the carpet. Piece by piece, the train tracks came out and lay on the carpet. The transformer and the connecting cord came out and were placed on the carpet. Special parts, like switches and signals, came out and were spread on the carpet.

Quietly, the mother said to the father, "Did you ever see them so wrapped up in anything? We sure must have made a good decision."

The father nodded and put his arm around his wife. "Sure looks that way, hon."

So mother went to the kitchen to check on the breakfast buns, and father went to the garage to check the oil in the car, preparatory to their planned visits later in the day, and the children were left to their own devices in the living room.

So, later, when the mother came to the garage to find her husband, he was surprised at the odd expression on her face. She stood looking at him for a moment, then said, "I think you ought to come and see what's happening."

His face showed his puzzlement. "It can't be that they hurt themselves, or you would be more hysterical. What's happening?"

She shook her head from side to side and smiled half-heartedly. "You have to see it to believe it. I saw it and I don't think I believe it even now."

So the husband closed the hood of the car, wiped his hands and followed his wife back through the kitchen into the house. Quietly they approached the archway into the living room and looked around the corner toward the area where the tree stood where the carpet was covered with gifts and paper, and where the children still were.

A squeal of glee came from Betty, whose back was to them, and an answering squeal came from Kenny. "That marble's too big! It can't hold on the track!" He collapsed in laughter.

The father inched around the corner to get a better view of what was happening. Piece by piece, the train tracks had been propped at various heights and angles on building blocks, which had been another gift for Kenny, and the tracks were now configured in the approximate shape of a roller coaster. A tall stack of blocks led the way to a shorter stack and a still shorter stack and so on around the carpet, with the tracks laid atop the blocks, and since they could not bend in the shape for which they were being laid out, they seemed to be temporarily attached with string and Christmas ribbon.

"Let me try again," Betty's voice sounded in a shrill, near giggle pitch. "I'll use the next smallest size marble!"

Marbles had been another gift from Santa. The father let his eyes roam from the makeshift roller coaster to the carpet beyond where the transformer, the railroad cars, the switches, the signals, and other paraphernalia still lay untouched.

As Betty placed the next marble at the top of the track and released it, it rolled quickly downward making a clicking sound whenever it crossed one of the ill-fitted connectors, curved, dipped, rose, curved again, leveled out and shot off the end of the last piece of track onto the carpet. Both children giggled convulsively.

"My turn! My turn!" Kenny screeched. And snatched up the marble which had just ended its journey, dashing back to the starting point.

The mother looked at the father. "Are they going to be inventors? Are they going to be engineers?"

The father chuckled softly and squeezed her hand. "Maybe they'll build amusement parks," he said, and kissed her forehead gently.

Christmas In Las Vegas

He had flown into Las Vegas on the afternoon of Christmas Eve. It was one of the few destinations for which seats could be obtained at short notice for Christmas Eve. Most people who wanted to make a holiday in Vegas would come in after the 25th, spending Christmas day somewhere else with their families

He hadn't wanted anyone to know where he was. He told the people in his office the day before that he was going to be out of town, and wished them a Merry Christmas. The office was closed today.

He didn't want his ex-wife to know where he was because she sometimes called him and nagged him about alimony. He had broken up with his girlfriend, probably irrevocably, and didn't want to stir the ashes of that relationship. No one else would want to know or care where he was.

Correction. A few creditors might want to know. Thank God for a few days of relief from that. Life had been depressing in recent times.

He had no one to spend Christmas with. On a previous trip to Vegas, he had made the acquaintance of a short, dimpled, large-busted waitress named Gina. When he decided to come to Vegas yesterday, he had called her and asked her if she wanted to spend Christmas with him. Her reply was hesitant, and he thought she sounded guilty.

"I have to spend Christmas with my husband this year. And my little boy."

"I thought you said your husband didn't live with you?"

Again he thought her voice sounded guilty. "But he's coming in for Christmas. He wants to spend Christmas with our little boy."

He knew a losing situation when he heard it, so he said he would give her a ring sometime later and wished her a Merry Christmas. He wondered if she had been lying about her husband not living with them.

After he got unpacked in his room, he had dinner in the hotel, played a few keno games, and went back to his room to freshen up. He thought he might get an early night's sleep, and called the hotel operator to leave a wakeup time. He turned on television and flicked through the channels.

The he took a deck of playing cards from his briefcase and, sitting on the bed, dealt himself imaginary poker hands and blackjack hands. After a while he swept up the cards and said, "Hell with it. I think I'll go downstairs."

The lounge show in the casino was loud and raucous. Its concession to the holiday season and the fact of Christmas Eve was three chorus girls wearing red Santa Claus caps, short red skirts with fur around the bottom, far above the knee, and bare breasts sprinkled with sequins. They had little bells in their hands and jingle bells fastened to their feet and they were dancing and singing a miserable version of "Here Comes Santa Claus."

He tried a few blackjack tables, winning and losing. As usual, losing a little more then winning.

He found a seat at a table in the poker room. Some of the other players looked like permanent losers who had no place else to go. Once he entertained that thought, it turned sour on him and he wondered how he looked to them.

After an hour, he decided it was late enough by Eastern Standard Time for him to be able to sleep. He cashed in his chips - only losing a little - and went back up to his room.

In the corridor on the way to his room, he was hustled by a middle-aged, fairly well dressed woman.

"Hi, sugar," she said in a simpering voice. "Want some company?"

He smiled and shook his head. "Not tonight, sweetheart. Maybe some other time." He wondered where her family was, if she had one. He locked his room door and, dropping on the bed, fell almost immediately asleep.

5:00 a.m. in Las Vegas is 8:00 a.m. on the east coast, and he was suddenly wide awake and feeling hungry. Putting on fresh shirt and slacks, he ran the electric razor over his jaw, splashed water on his face and headed back down to the hotel's main level.

The elevator played recorded Christmas music, and the thought struck him that it was Christmas morning. This fact was reinforced visually by the almost empty casino and, when he headed into the all night restaurant, the scarcity of patrons there. On a normal night, it would be busy at any hour.

He kidded with the waitress about what she had done to deserve duty on Christmas morning. She told him that what she had done was to be the last one hired.

There are no clocks in Las Vegas hotels, and especially not in the casino areas. Management doesn't want anyone to be distracted by a sense of time pressure. "No calendars either," he thought wryly. He checked his watch, thinking, "Carry my own hour of the day and day of the month on this little sucker. That'll show them," he thought, then was embarrassed by his sense of pettiness.

Back in the casino, he found a couple of blackjack tables open, and began to play methodically. Methodically he lost a little bit at a time. When he saw this pattern continuing, he took his remaining chips and moved to the one poker table that was in action.

Some of the same losers were there from the night before. They simply hadn't gone home. or wherever it was that they might go if they left the casino. He had seen poker players stay at a table for 24 hours or more. Again he looked at the people seated around the table.

Again he wondered, if these looked like losers to him, what might be their impression of him. With that thought still stinging, he made a rash bet when he should have folded. And he lost.

Suddenly, as he examined his hole cards for the next hand, he became aware of a public address voice repeating its announced request. "Mr. Rollins. Will Mr. Rollins please go to the house phone for a message. Mr. Rollins." He looked up and flicked his eyes around the table. Of course none of them knew he was Mr. Rollins.

His first reaction was to ignore the call. Or to hope there was some other Mr. Rollins in the casino area. With the few people of any description still there, he thought the odds against that were quite long.

Finally he rose from the table, "Save my place here." As he hurried to look for a house phone, his mind whirled.

"How can anybody know I'm here? I didn't tell anybody. Not anybody. I just said I'd be out of town. Gina thinks my name is Roberts. Nobody can know I'm here. Surely on Christmas day the IRS isn't going to run me down." He found the house phone and picked it up.

The operator said, "Yes?"

He said, "This is Rollins. You paged me."

There was a pause while the operator looked at her list of messages. "Oh!" Her voice took on a different tone. "We're glad to know you are all right, Mr. Rollins."

He looked at the phone. "What makes you say that? I'm all right."

The operator's voice came into his ear. "Well Mr. Rollins, you left a wakeup call for this morning, and you didn't answer it. We tried you several times. And so we were just afraid you might be sick or something had happened. We're glad to know you're fine."

He laughed. "Forgot about the wakeup call. Sorry to bother you." He looked again at the phone and then said in a more ingratiating tone, "And thanks for the call. Thanks for worrying."

"No trouble Mr. Rollins. Oh, and Merry Christmas to you!"

He held the phone momentarily and then said, "Yes. Merry Christmas to you, too."

He cradled the phone slowly, his eyes staring at his hand still holding the receiver. "An operator has to wish me Merry Christmas, and only because I didn't answer my phone." He dropped his hand and turned back to survey the nearly empty casino. "I've got to get my life together." His tone was half anxious, half surprised. After a moment, he headed back to the poker table.

The Buck Rogers
Rocket Ship

When the grandboys came to visit for the Christmas holidays, Grandpa Alex had one special treat in mind for them.

Because in the city where Grandpa Alex and Grandma Rose lived there was a wonderful toy museum. It was said to be the largest and most complete collection of antique toys and dolls in the world.

And they were having a special show of toys of the nineteen thirties. And since Grandpa Alex had been a little boy in the thirties, he wanted to show the grandkids the kind of toys that he had gotten at Christmases many years ago.

In order to interest the kids, called Kipper and Nipper by their parents and so by their grandparents, Grandpa Alex had to downplay to the point of nonmention the fact that a large portion of the museum was devoted to dolls. He stressed the fact that there were some of the greatest toys in the world on display, and that there would be things they had never seen anyplace else.

Kipper and Nipper, being seven and eight respectively, had their doubts that there was any toy they hadn't seen. But they were willing to be convinced. Grandpa also had to prepare them psychologically in advance for the idea that toys of the past were not radio controlled, were not computer controlled, and did not involve video activities.

This seem to tickle the fancy of Kipper and Nipper more than anything else they had heard. "You mean," said Kipper, "that nothing was remote controlled? How did you control it, then?"

Grandpa Alex laughed. "A lot of times, you didn't control it. That was part of the fun."

"Wow!" said Nipper. "Does that ever sound cool."

So the appointed day between Christmas and New Year's arrived, and Grandpa Alex and Kipper and Nipper went to the toy museum. Grandpa carefully steered them in the direction from the entrance which would avoid the doll wing of the museum.

Feeling that he was being steered, Kipper, the older and wiser of the two, craned his head back in the direction from which they were being led. "What's back there, Grandpa?"

"That's where all the dolls are, guys. I didn't think you'd want to see that, so we are going straight to the toys."

"Well," said Kipper, casting a sidelong glance at his brother, "it might not hurt us just to see what they look like. Guys ought to know about stuff. Right Nipper?" Nipper nodded. "Yeh. But let's see the toys first."

So they proceeded into a wonderland of children's pasts. Kipper and Nipper were delighted at every turn. The only thing that disappointed them a little was that most things were in glass cases, and could be looked at, and the glass could be smeared with fingermarks, but the toys couldn't actually be touched.

As they wandered through from room to room and from display to display, they came to what, for Grandpa Alex, was the piece de resistance - the toys of the thirties display. He carefully explained to the boys that these were actually like the toys that he had gotten as Christmas presents and birthday presents and had played with when he was their age.

The boys enjoyed this room just as they had enjoyed the others. But to Grandpa Alex, it was his childhood revisited. At every turn he saw something that he had forgotten or something that he had anticipated seeing and rekindling fond memories from.

The day flashed by, and at last they were through with every display on the entire floor.

"Gee, Grandpa, that was really swell, that was really great," Kipper said. "Yeh, neato," Nipper chimed in.

Grandpa was looking around in a seemingly aimless fashion and he slowed to a stop. "What's wrong, Grandpa?" Nipper asked.

Alex still looked around him in some dismay. "You know, guys," he said. "There's one toy that was really big time when I was a kid and that I don't see here at all. I don't see how they can have a museum and not have that in it."

Kipper looked up at his grandfather. "Well, if it was really important, it ought to be here. What was it Grandpa?"

"Yeh, what was it?" Nipper chimed in.

"It was the Buck Rogers rocketship," Grandpa Alex said in a voice filled with reverence. "It was the greatest toy I ever had."

Kipper looked at him with some doubt. "What was Buck Rogers? And why was a rocketship so special?"

"Yeh, why?" Nipper said.

Grandpa said, "Let's sit on this bench for a minute boys. It's been a long walk around here. And I'll tell you."

They sat, and Alex said, "You see, boys, back in those days, there weren't any rocketships. There weren't any. There weren't any spaceships. There weren't any missiles. There weren't any rockets."

Kipper stared intently at Alex. "So how could they have a rocketship toy?"

Alex looked at the boys. "Because, boys," he said, "because somebody made it up. A writer invented the idea of a rocketship before there ever was a rocketship. It was a cartoon. It was a comic strip. It was in the daily papers. Buck Rogers. And he was in the future, and he had a rocketship and he went to the stars and the other planets."

Kipper and Nipper stared at their grandfather. "You really mean it, Grandpa? They made it up before there every was such a thing? They really did?"

Grandpa nodded. "Yes, they really did."

"Wow, wow!" Nipper said.

"Yes, Grandpa," Kipper said, "but it's not here. If it was really real, it would be here." He looked more intently at Grandpa Alex. "Maybe you made it up, Grandpa?"

Grandpa shook his head emphatically. "I may be old, boys, but I haven't lost my brains yet. I'm telling you the facts. The only fact that I don't know is why they don't have it here."

"Well," said Kipper, "I guess we're rested. We probably oughtta just take a peek at those old dolls."

Alex laughed and stood taking the boys hands. "Okay guys. Let's just peek in at those old dolls."

They retraced their steps, going back down the corridor through which they had entered the toy section of the museum, and found their way back to the lobby from which the entrance to the other wing could be seen. And as they were walking across the lobby, suddenly they came to a single, tall slender glass case in the center of the lobby. There was only one shelf in the glass case and there was only one item on display.

It was the Buck Rogers rocketship.

Alex and the boys saw it at the same time. Alex's eyes widened in surprise, and the boys jumped up and down.

"Wow, wow, Grandpa Alex," Nipper said. "It's really here!"

"Yeh, wow!" Kipper said, his voice bubbling with enthusiasm. "And it was so important that they put it out here in the front all by itself!"

Nipper looked up at his grandfather in awe. "Yeh, Grandpa." He continued to stare at Alex, his head bent back. "It really was a Buck Rogers rocketship. And they really did imagine it. And you really told us the truth."

Grandpa Alex smiled. "Yes boys. I really did."

So they headed off to check out the dolls.

The Office Party

Rachel hated the way many of the girls in the various headquarters offices behaved. She felt they were overly bold, overly aggressive, and pushing the bounds of acceptable behavior.

She knew some of the men did this too, and she hated it as well. But she had grown up knowing that men behaved that way. And she had never felt that women should exhibit some of the bad characteristics of men.

And now it was the afternoon of the Christmas office party, and she dreaded to think of what was to follow.

She had been tempted to find an excuse not to go. Then she had thought it would be embarrassing to explain why she didn't think the office party was fun or good for morale. Then she had decided that she probably had to go. Already, her stomach was rumbling in anticipation of future events.

Now she was in the ladies' room to check her hair and makeup, and the room was filled with other chattering women, most of them young. She watched three or four lined up at the mirror, adding to their blue eyelid shadow. She disliked it intensely, and thought it not appropriate for work.

As she waited her turn at the mirror, she saw many dresses whose skirts she considered too short, or whose necklines she considered too daring, or both.

She told herself that maybe some of the girls had dressed for the party rather than for the work day. But shouldn't it have been the other way?

"Weil, girls," said a stocky dark-haired girl, as she touched up her rouge and lipstick, "you ready for the annual feel-up?"

One of the other girls giggled. "Isn't that sexual harassment nowadays?"

The first girl laughed. "Only if you don't feel back." The room erupted in uproarious laughter. Rachel felt her cheeks grow pink, and she turned away.

As she finally got to use the mirror, she thought her hair looked nice. Maybe too conservative, by many of these girls' standards. Looking into her eyes in the mirror, she liked their blue-grey hue. To herself, she wondered, "Am I too repressed? Or are these girls really acting out against their own insecurities?"

She knew they would drink, as, of course, would the men. She knew untoward things would happen. She hated it all. But, as she was leaving the ladies room, heading back toward her own work area, she had another thought. "Am I feeling this way because of Jeff Bernam? Am I upset because I don't want him being a part of this kind of stuff?"

Walking down the hall, she thought of Jeff, the accounting supervisor. Because of her job, she had to bring work to him at least once a day. She was desperately in love with him. At least she could acknowledge that.

On the other hand, she doubted that he had any thoughts about her except that she brought work to him every day, and it was usually done right. What she saw as the ethics of office behavior might cause him never to know - because she could never tell him - of her true emotional feelings.

Other girls would shamelessly angle for dates with other men in the office, and the men would respond if they wanted to. Sometimes, she reflected ruefully, even if they were married. And, she admitted, sometimes the women were married.

She shook her head, frowning angrily. "Some of them have no shame at all," she thought. "Almost no morals at all," she thought. "I wonder why I keep on working here."

A few more steps and she turned into her work area. "You know why," she told herself. "It's because if you didn't work here, you'd never see Jeff Bernam."

She sat at her desk. Still musing, she thought, "Or maybe if I didn't work here, I'd just call him up one day and ask him if he wanted to go out on a date. Shameless." She made aimless circles on the desktop with her finger. "And he'd say no, and that would be the miserable end of that," she thought.

One of the girls walked up and down the halls ringing a bell. It sounded like a cowbell. From previous years, Rachel knew that this was the conventional signal for work to stop on the afternoon of a party. Sometimes they had parties for people's birthdays or retirements. But the only serious big party was the last work day before Christmas.

Reluctantly, she gathered her papers and put them into a pile to be worked after the holiday. She stood, straightening her skirt, and headed down the hallway to the conference room. She knew it was festively decorated, because she had been by it earlier and seen other girls working on it.

By the time she reached the room, it was filled with perhaps sixty or seventy people, about two-thirds of them female. Some volunteers were ladling out punch, for those who didn't go to the sideboard where the liquor and ice were available. The top of the conference table was covered with paper tablecloths in Christmas colors, and paper plates full of many kinds of cookies, nuts, fruits, and sweets.

Most of the people already had drinks and were milling around. Rachel pushed her way to the punch bowl and accepted a Christmas-decorated cup. Then she backed away and tried to get into a noncongested spot.

There were no noncongested spots. So she stood with one of the other girls whom she thought of as conservative, and surveyed the scene. Already, there were flagrant evidences of flirtations, often initiated by women, since there were substantially more women then men.

But, from experience, she thought she knew who the wolves were, and she watched three or four of the men already becoming obnoxious with drink and what she imagined, without hearing, to be aggressive propositions.

She looked for Jeff Bernam. He should have been easy to spot since he was taller than average and had wavy red hair. She surveyed the room twice and still did not spot him. "He must be coming in late, or else he got a last minute phone call," she thought.

One of the older men approached her, said a few pleasantries, offered to refill her drink. She smiled, said no thanks, and noticed that he was pressing very close to her and that his arm, seemingly accidentally, was nevertheless firmly pressed against her bosom. She quickly backed away and moved to another part of the room.

From where she stood now, she was near the entrance door. She looked again around the room and couldn't see any evidence of Jeff. She thought she might just duck down the hall, see if he was still in his office, and remind him that the party was going on. That surely was pretty innocent, wasn't it? Or was it?

Nevertheless, after a brief hesitation, she did just that, carrying her punch cup with her. Down the hall and around the corner she could see his outer office door. She approached it, then walked through it and toward the inner office, just as she did every day, delivering her report.

She saw no lights, but her momentum carried her forward, and almost compulsively, she looked through the inner door. There was Jeff, tall, his hair only barely distinguishable in the unlighted room, with his arms wrapped tightly around one of the office women. There lips were fastened in a seeming unending kiss. Rachel didn't know how long she stood before forcing herself to back away.

She ran back to her office, threw her cup into the wastebasket, grabbed her coat off the hook and ran toward the elevator. She was angry at herself, furious at Jeff, even more furious at the woman who she considered a slut, and shaking so badly she could barely find the arms of her coat as she angrily punched the elevator button again.

She was alone in the elevator as it descended. She felt a great hollowness following the anger. "I'll resign next week," she told herself. "I hate it here. I don't know how I could have been so stupid. I don't know how he could've been so stupid. I don't know how she could do that. I don't know how he could let her do that." Her mind tumbled over and over with these thoughts. The recurring principal one was, "How can I be so stupid?"

As she stepped out of the lobby into the street, she saw that snow was falling. Beside the lobby door, a man dressed in a Santa Claus suit rang a bell and supervised a cauldron for charitable donations. Blindly, she fished into her purse, pulled out a dollar bill and stuffed it into the cauldron, turning away toward the subway. "Merry Christmas!" the bell-ringing Santa called. "Happy New Year!"

She bowed her head, facing into the snow. She hoped she could reach the subway entrance before her high heels slipped on the snowy sidewalk.

Santa Has Many Helpers

Hans Wilhelm liked to say he had four distinctions. When asked, he would enumerate them thus: (1.) He was born in Germany, but had become an American citizen, and had fought for the Americans in the war; (2.) He was a master carpenter; (3.) He had an enormous belly; and (4.) Each December he played Santa Claus.

December was his favorite month. And he played his favorite role of Santa as often as he could. But never for pay.

He volunteered his services and his costume to as many different charitable groups and community service groups as could fit into his schedule. His services were in demand, both because he bore no cost, and because he was very good.

The Lions Clubs had first call on him because he was a Lion. But the Kiwanis and the Rotary and the Optimists and the American Legion and the religious-related organizations and the ethnic organizations, like the Sons of Italy, - all these and more were on his schedule when they could be fitted in.

And this particular December, December 18th, was his big day. Of course, sometimes the biggest day would fall on a different date, depending on what day of the month Thursday was. One would think Saturday would be a big day, and sometimes it was, but on the average, Thursday was it, because so many groups met that day. And this year, Thursday was December the 18th.

Hans had a Santa appearance at a breakfast club meeting. Then a local civic association had a morning function. Then there was a noon Rotary club meeting. So far, none of these had directly involved children, but instead either collection of gifts for children, or distribution of gifts among club members, and sometimes planning for a future children's event.

Then came the afternoon. He attended a planning meeting with a committee of the town council, preparing for the party in town park which would be on Saturday. After that, he was scheduled for an after-school party sponsored by a combination of civic groups, primarily for underprivileged children. Then there would be a dinner meeting of another service club, which was for families, and where he would be especially expected to shine when he made his appearance, to the delight of the children, after dinner.

So, because of the tightness of his schedule, Hans found it necessary to wear his Santa costume from morning to night.

The only time when it might not be appropriate was at the planning meeting with the city council members. But when he arrived there at 2:30, he explained that he had to leave at 3:30 for the underprivileged children party. The council members smiled and nodded, and the mayor extended his hand.

Extending his hand was a move the mayor regretted very soon thereafter, because Hans had a tremendously strong grip, and never seemed to realize the discomfort he caused other adults when shaking their hands. But his smile and infectious laughter and jiggling belly redeemed him, and the mayor, quickly placing his hand behind his back, welcomed Hans and gestured to the seat reserved for him.

But, a few minutes later, as the mayor opened his folder and prepared to begin the meeting, he became aware of something distressing. He looked up at Hans, who was leaning back in his chair.

Beneath his Santa beard, Hans' face was a sickly gray, in marked contrast to its usual ruddiness. His hands were holding what would have been his chest, were it not for his enormous expanse of belly.

"Mr. Wilhelm," the mayor said anxiously, "is something wrong? Can we help you?" Immediately, the other men and women at the table, once they had looked at Hans, were alarmed. Several of them rose as if to offer personal help.

Hans' eyes seemed to be squinted in pain. He gasped out, "Maybe it vas somting at lunch. Maybe indichestion." He continued to hold his front.

"Maybe something worse," whispered the commissioner at the mayor's left. The mayor nodded distractedly, not taking his eyes from Hans' face.

"I tink I be all right," Hans said in a strained voice.

A worried woman near the end of the table, head of a civic association, said, "Mr. Wilhelm, why doesn't one of us take you home? You'll probably feel better lying down." Her tone showing her concern.

Hans slowly moved his head from side to side. "I got the underprivileged kids today. Then I got the Lions Clubs families and their kids. Not today." His head shook again from side to side. "Not today, I don't go home."

"Well," the mayor said dubiously, "at least I'm going to get one of the town workers to drive you to the underprivileged kids party, I'm going to have him stay with you, and he's going to drive you to the Lions party, and he's going to stay with you. You're in no shape to drive."

Hans' voice showed his embarrassment. "Vat special treatment! Vy am I so special?" Then he laughed weakly. "I know. It is Santa who is so special. Only because I am Santa." He repeated his weak laugh. "But only because it is Santa, I let you do dis. And I tank you."

The mayor hurried out, found the maintenance supervisor, and had him escort Hans slowly from the room into the maintenance worker's vehicle.

The supervisor, who, like many others in the town, knew Hans, watched his work at the underprivileged childrens' party.

Hans moved slowly, but he seemed excellent in his duties with the children. In the supervisor's eyes, it seemed the party would never end. But at last it did.

The children cheered and clapped for Santa's performance, wished him well, waved and yelled, "Come back next year, Santa!"

So they went to the Lions dinner. The banquet room was packed, about half of those present, so it seemed, were children. Hans declined to eat, partly because he needed to stay out of sight until his part of the program following dinner, and partly because, as he said to the supervisor, 'I don't tink I eat any more today. I tink eating maybe did dis."

So the supervisor sat with Hans in an anteroom, concealed from the children, and didn't eat either. And when they heard the club president on the public address system announcing the after-dinner special treat for the kids, the supervisor helped Hans stand and waited to open the door for his grand entrance.

The program was a huge success. The club president said so, the maintenance supervisor thought so, and the children certainly thought so. Standing close enough to listen, the supervisor heard conversations like this:

"This year I want a Barbie doll," said the little girl sitting on Santa's knee. Santa patted her back. "Vell, ve see about that. I hope ve can. Merry Christmas!"

"Merry Christmas, Santa!" the little girl said and ran back to her mother and father at their table.

Children were lined up half around the room, and one by one they came to talk to Santa. One child expressed doubt.

"I don't think you're the real Santa," he said. "How can Santa be everywhere?"

Hans looked at the young boy through his Santa eyebrows and over his Santa spectacles. "You very smart young man. You right, there's one main Santa. But Santa has many helpers. I am also a Santa. He is Santa Claus. His helpers have other names." He looked into the young boy's eyes. "I," he said, "am Santa Wilhelm." He pronounced it Vilhelm.

The boy looked at him in awe. "Gee," he said. "I guess I just never thought about that. Sure. It's like a bunch of brothers. They're all called the same last name but they have different first names." He stilled looked into Han's eyes. "But in Santa's family, they all have the same first name."

Hans nodded his head, "Yes, young man. You're very smart. All Santa's helpers have the same first name - Santa. Santa has many helpers." He patted the boy and sent him back to his parents.

At last the long line was at an end, and Santa, pale behind his beard, was cheered by the parents, the club members, and the children together. The maintenance supervisor helped Santa to make his exit.

The next day, rushed to a hospital, Hans died. His doctor determined the cause to have been a heart attack. Hundreds of people, children and adults, mourned for Hans Wilhelm. All remembered him in his role as Santa. His going left an empty feeling in their hearts.

After the memorial service, the maintenance supervisor walked with mayor toward their cars. "But, you know," the supervisor said. "I keep remembering what Hans told that kid, 'Santa has many helpers', he told the kid." The mayor looked at him.

"It's like," the supervisor added, "It's like he meant Christmas will go on, you know?"

The mayor nodded. They had reached the parking lot. "Santa has many helpers," he repeated softly.

The Christmas Necktie

It was the last day of classes for students at Southeast High before the Christmas vacation began. Mr. Kenyon had planned to read a story to his English classes, to make the last day less demanding and more pleasant for the students.

The first two periods had gone well. When the bell rang to begin the third period, students moved to their desks and Mr. Kenyon looked dubiously at the tall, slovenly boy who moved to the front desk in the row by the windows. Wilbur March had almost a perfect zero for his work in the fall semester.

Wilbur never seemed to have textbooks with him. Today, he was carrying a long flat box, about four inches wide, ten inches long and three quarters of an inch high. This he laid carefully on his desk, squaring it with the corner of the desktop, then folded his hands and looked out the window.

Mr. Kenyon read the story for the third time, and elicited a largely pleased reaction from the girls and boys who seemed to hang onto his words. He congratulated himself on his reading style, and then dismissed the class. Wilbur March remained seated.

Mr. Kenyon looked at him, then said, "Class is over, Wilbur. I hope you have a good holiday."

Wilbur slowly lifted his lanky form from the desk, picked up the box, and extended it to his teacher.

"Merry Christmas to you Mr. Kenyon," Wilbur said in a diffident voice. "I hope you enjoy your holiday."

The teacher looked at the box, not taking it. "That's for me?"

Wilbur nodded, extending it again. Through the teacher's mind ran the principal's admonition that teachers should not solicit gifts nor imply that they expected them. At the same time, he did not wish to antagonize further this hopelessly failing student.

"Thank you, Wilbur. Merry Christmas again." He took the box and laid it on his desk at the front of the room. Wilbur smiled momentarily and turned to leave the room.

When John Kenyon got home at the end of the day, he kissed his wife, said, "Happy holiday. Thank God."

His wife laughed. "Glad to have you home for a few days."

The teacher, removing his coat remembered the flat box in his pocket and pulled it out, extending it toward Mrs.

Kenyon. "Guess what? Guess who gave me a gift? Obviously unsolicited."

"Who?"

"My most hopeless failing student."

His wife nodded, "Wilbur March, right?"

"Yes. It's a necktie. I opened it. Take a look."

Mrs. Kenyon lifted the lid of the box and looked at the very colorful necktie pattern. She looked up, "He probably thinks it's gorgeous."

Her husband laughed. "I hope so. Otherwise, maybe he thinks he's getting back at me."

She laid the gift near the still undecorated tree which they would work on that evening.

At dinner, she looked at her husband. "John."

He looked up from his meal. "Yes, dear? What is it?"

She studied her napkin. "Do you think Wilbur March would try to bribe you to get a passing grade? By giving you a Christmas gift?"

John Kenyon shook his head. "Gosh, I can't think he would do that. He has to know he's failing." He continued to stare at his plate. After a silence, he said, "I guess I'm conceited enough to hope he gave it to me because he liked me." He paused again. "But you raise a disturbing thought. That would really bother me if he did that."

Almost every day thereafter, during the Christmas vacation, John Kenyon would let his eyes wander to the flat box under the tree. And every day he would have a sinking feeling that his student had expected to curry favor and even to get a passing grade. The more he thought about it, the more he was disturbed. He didn't know what he would say or do when school began again.

On the first day after the vacation, as third period rolled around, John's mind was again on Wilbur March. And, as the students filed into the room, the tall gangling Wilbur shuffled to the front and stopped at the teacher's desk.

Before John Kenyon could speak, Wilbur extended a piece of paper toward him. "Please sign my withdrawal, Mr. Kenyon."

John Kenyon looked at the paper. "What's this about?"

Wilbur still held the paper forward. "I'm transferring to a private school where they will let me be eligible for basketball. Basketball is the only thing I'm interested in, Mr. Kenyon."

The teacher looked up. "So you're leaving now?"

"Yes. Their semester starts tomorrow." After a pause Wilbur added, "Thank you for being decent to me, Mr. Kenyon. I know I didn't try. I always knew I was going to leave. You didn't hassle me like some of the others. Thanks again."

John Kenyon signed the paper, saying nothing. He handed it back to Wilbur who took it. Still the teacher was silent.

"Well, thanks again Mr. Kenyon. Hope you liked your tie. Be seeing you around." He turned and moved toward the door.

The teacher still stood at his desk. Finally he said, "And a Happy New Year to you, Wilbur." As Wilbur looked back, the teacher added, "And good luck."

When Wilbur was gone and the students were settling at their desks, John Kenyon murmured softly, "And I like the tie better now."

Christmas In Two Houses

Cindy and Jonathon sat in their apartment in Manhattan, looking at their small tree which they had just finished decorating. "Not bad," Jonathon said.

Cindy jumped up. "Well, onward and upward. Time to get to mom's." She went to the closet for her coat.

Jonathon pulled on his coat and turned off the lights. "You know," he said, "it's kind of lucky that your mom and your family traditionally exchange gifts and have their Christmas dinner on Christmas Eve."

Cindy looked up at him as they both stooped to pick up shopping bags of gifts from the entrance hall. "Well," she said, "that's just how they do it."

They walked out into the elevator hallway. As Jonathon locked the door behind them he said, "Yeah, but what I'm getting at is that it gives me a chance to be with your family, and then and go be with my mom and dad on Christmas day. It really works out good."

Cindy punched the elevator button. "I wish I could go with you to see them, too."

He nodded. "But you see them other times. And your mother's alone, so she needs you on Christmas."

The elevator door opened and they stepped in. Cindy nodded as she punched the button for the ground floor. "I know. You know how I am. I like to try to do everything." She laughed.

He hugged her and kissed her forehead. "You do almost everything," he laughed.

Late that night, the dinner and the festivities over, the family reunion, in effect, completed, Jonathon and Cindy lay in bed. She looked up into the darkness.

"I'm going to miss you tomorrow, Jon. I always miss you when you're gone."

"I'll be back the next day," he said as he brought his lips against hers. When she responded only slightly, he lowered his lips to her shoulders, her breasts, and on down her body. Gradually she grew more responsive until they were wrapped passionately in each others arms.

Jonathon caught the earliest plane out on Christmas morning to Washington. It was only half filled, because many of those who would travel on Christmas day would still be asleep. He saw the city recede behind him as the plane climbed in elevation, then he settled down to read until an hour later he watched the descent into Washington.

He caught a cab to where he kept a car garaged for his use when he was in Washington and for when he visited his parents. He had brought a shopping bag full of gifts for his parents, in addition to ones that had been shipped earlier. These he placed on the floor behind the driver's seat. Before backing the car out of its garage, he checked the trunk. The other shopping bag of gifts which he had placed there earlier in the month was still intact. He slammed the lid, returned to the driver's seat, and backed the car out into the street.

A few minutes later, he had the shopping bag from the trunk and was ringing the bell of an apartment in a suburban Washington highrise.

The door was opened by a stunning dark haired woman still in her robe. Her face broke into a brilliant smile and she held out her arms. "Jon, I hadn't expected you for at least another hour!"

Jonathon dropped the shopping bag and wrapped the woman in his arms. Their bodies melted together in a tight embrace, and his lips sought hers.

Minutes later, they were together in her bed, unclothed and joined in intimate embrace.

When she could catch her breath, she said, "Thank you for coming on Christmas. I know it's hard. My day would have been terrible without you here."

He rested his head on her shoulder, his eyes focused on her erect nipple. "You know I see you when I can, Robin." He laughed. "That's why I catch the first plane out."

She pulled him back into her embrace.

In mid-afternoon, he rang the bell at his parents apartment, and his mother opened the door. She broke into a smile which was as bright as the Christmas decorations she wore on the shoulder of her dress.

"Son, we wondered when you'd get here. We were hoping it was earlier. But naturally we're glad to see you." She hugged him and he hugged in return. Behind them, his father came out, assisted by a cane. He reached behind his mother to shake his father's hand.

"Come in son," his father said. "We've got some good food we've been holding here. Bring that bag and get your coat off."

At Cindy's mother's house, Cindy sat stirring her coffee. Her mother was heating coffeecake in the microwave. "Mom," Cindy said, I hope I'm wrong. Somehow I just feel maybe Jon has another woman."

Her mother looked at her, studying her. She turned back to the microwave, counting the seconds down. "Don't look for trouble, dear. Trouble comes too often without our having to look for it."

Cindy nodded, and raised her cup to her lips. "I know. I know I shouldn't look for trouble. It's just a feeling that I have sometimes."

When Jonathon had gone from his parents' house to catch the early morning plane on the day after Christmas, his parents sat in the kitchen over a second cup of coffee. As his mother stirred, hers she looked out into the early morning darkness.

"You know, dear," she said softly, "I somehow have the feeling that Jonathon has another woman."

Her husband looked up, raising his eyebrows. "What?"

She continued stirring her coffee. "It's just a feeling that I have. You know how sometimes you just get a feeling?"

He took a sip of his coffee, and then set the cup back into the saucer. "Don't look for trouble." He looked into his wife's eyes. "That's a motto of mine. That's something that I think we have been able to live with very well. Don't look for trouble."

She nodded. "I know, I know."

Sunrise came late on December mornings. As the plane took off over Washington, Jonathon could barely make out the icy covering of the reflecting pool next to the Washington Monument. "Probably too thin to skate on," he thought. As the plane climbed over Washington, in the pre-dawn, he could still see the Christmas lights spread out like a giant web across the city. And as the plane climbed the lights became smaller and finally disappeared behind him.

"I guess I'm on thin ice," he told himself, thinking of the reflecting pool. He stared out into the darkness. "I wonder when I'm going to get myself into trouble?"

He still stared into the darkness which, now turned pearl grey as the sun was near the horizon. "Or," he told himself, "maybe I'm already in it."

The Monopoly Game

Elsie and Bob were a young couple who lived next door to nine-year old Ricky and his parents. Among other things, Elsie and Bob liked to take their boat out on the lake, go to the golf club, and go to the movies.

They also liked to play Monopoly.

Ricky liked to walk Elsie's and Bob's bull terrier, Caesar, because this usually led to a reward of candy in some form. So, on this December day, when Ricky brought Caesar back from his walk, and came with him into Elsie's and Bob's kitchen, he saw through the entryway into the dining room that Elsie and Bob were setting up their Monopoly board. Quickly giving Caesar a dog biscuit, Ricky rushed in to the dining room table.

"Please let me play! Please let me play! Please let me play!" Ricky said breathlessly, his face alight with excitement.

Elsie looked up at him through her blond bangs. "Do you know how to play, Ricky?" She asked dubiously.

"Ricky doesn't know how to play," Bob said dismissively.

"Yes I do! Yes I do!" Ricky's voice rose an octave and his eyes grew brighter. Elsie turned her blue eyes toward Bob. "Maybe we could let him try."

"Great! Great! You haven't really started yet. Just count out another set of money! I'll be the purple piece."

Bob looked at Elsie, his eyes narrowed. "You think so?"

"Okay, I'll be the orange piece," Ricky said pulling up a chair.

Elsie's eyes locked with Bob's. "I think so. See how it goes."

So the game began. Ricky's enthusiasm was unbridled. Whenever he landed on something which could be bought, he bought it with great exuberance. When he had finally assembled a matching set of low-priced properties, he built houses as soon as he was able.

Elsie and Bob methodically rolled their dice, bought their properties, paid their fees, and waited patiently each time it was Ricky's turn.

There was an open two-pound box of chocolates on Elsie's side of the table. Seeing Ricky's eyes dart frequently in that direction, she pushed the box across the table. "Like to have a chocolate, Ricky?"

Bob's eyes turned to Elsie. In a low voice he said, "Chocolate fingers?"

"Gosh yes, Ms. Elsie!" Ricky touched three bonbons before selecting the one to bite into. "Thanks a lot!"

Caesar came in from the kitchen and sat up on his hind legs beside Ricky's chair, his forefeet dangling in front of his chest, begging. Ricky looked down. "Can Caesar have one?"

"No," Bob said.

Elsie's eyes widened as she looked quickly at Bob. "Maybe just one, Bob?" "Gosh yes, Ms. Elsie," Ricky said enthusiastically. "Caesar's a good boy. He deserves one!"

Selecting a bonbon he had not touched previously, Ricky began to lift it from the box, changed his mind, and selected another one. This one he held out away from the table in the direction of the begging dog. Ricky dropped the chocolate toward Caesar. Caesar missed it.

"Gosh I'm sorry!" Ricky jumps up. "I didn't think he'd miss it!"

He stepped in the direction of the dog, and, as Elsie watched in horror, his foot squashed the bonbon on the light tan carpet. "Oh no!" Ricky said in agony. "Oh no!" Elsie said, almost in unison.

"What? What?" Bob asked apprehensively.

"I'll get a towel," Ricky said, turning toward the kitchen.

"Get paper napkins," Elsie called quickly. "We don't want to ruin a towel."

"What? What?" Bob asked urgently again.

As Ricky was entering the kitchen, he heard Elsie say, "You don't want to know. It has to do with a chocolate."

When Ricky returned with the napkins, he succeed in smearing the chocolate into a wider dark brown smudge. Elsie jumped up and said, "Don't touch it any more! I have something that might help take it out." She ran into the kitchen.

Bob raised himself from his side of the table and peered over the edge. "Oh my God."

At last the game resumed, a somewhat dimmer and less defined brown smudge remaining on the carpet, and Caesar banished to the kitchen. Bob surveyed the board. "Looks like it's about time for me to bankrupt you guys. Sure took long enough with all the interruptions."

But he couldn't bankrupt Ricky, because Ricky, through a miraculous series of rolls, refused to land on any of Bob's properties. Ricky had sold his houses, mortgaged some of his properties, and had only three small rent-collectors left in operation.

Elsie still had improved property on the board, and was desperately trying to recoup. Each roll of the dice became more of a hazardous undertaking.

She rolled, and landed on a Chance square, avoiding Bob's property. Ricky rolled and landed on Go, collecting $200. Bob rolled and counted spaces. His piece landed on one of Ricky's remaining unimproved properties.

Ricky leaped to his feet in excitement. "Oh oh! Oh oh! That'll be $12!"

Bob looked pained. "This is holding up the game," he muttered, mostly to himself, counting out a ten and two ones.

"Thank you! Thank you!" Ricky accepted the money.

The game ground to its inevitable end, with Bob the winner. Ricky jumped up. guess I better go home now. I don't think my mom knows where I am." He hurried to the door.

"Goodbye, Ricky," Bob said.

On Christmas morning, Ricky went to the front door to look at the new-fallen snow. As he pulled the inner door open, a package which had been wedged between it and the storm door tipped over and fell into the foyer. It was wrapped in Christmas paper.

Ricky carried it into the living room, where his mother and father were surveying the wreckage of gifts already opened. As he tore the paper from the package in his hands, revealing the contents, he shouted excitedly, "Look Mom! Look Dad! It's from Ms. Elsie and Mr. Bob." He held the package toward them.

"It's a Monopoly game!"

Mother Comes Home

We wanted mother home for Christmas. Stricken with a serious heart attack early in December, she had been hospitalized, mainly in intensive care, in the intervening days. Now it was two days before Christmas.

I asked my husband to talk to the heart specialist, hoping the doctor would allow her to leave the hospital. Somehow I felt that an older person should be home - that anybody should be home for that matter - if they can find it possible at a time like Christmas. This season had always meant so much to her.

So when my husband Rick drove into the garage, I was waiting for him in the kitchen, my hopes and fears both high. When he opened the door from the garage, I searched his face looking for something - some expression, to justify my hope.

He looked at me for a moment, then said, "Well. Good news and bad news."

Sometimes my husband can be very aggravating indeed. "Don't tear me up with suspense. Tell me what the doctor said."

He smiled. "I'm sorry. But it is good news and bad news." He paused. "The doctor says we can bring her home tomorrow morning. That's Christmas Eve. He says they wouldn't be doing any more procedures for a couple of days anyway, as long as nothing changes for the worse. And the hospital is kind of understaffed and halfway shut down at Christmas anyway."

A smile began at the corners of my mouth. "So that's good news. She can come home tomorrow. Christmas Eve."

He nodded but he didn't smile. "Yes. But the bad news is he thinks she's so frail and that her condition is so bad that any little thing could cause a setback and maybe another attack."

I stared at him and then shrugged. "But that could happen when they are taking her to the bathroom in the hospital or when they are wheeling her down for x-rays, or when they are making her get up in her chair."

He nodded. "Yes. And I know you want her home. And I do too." He went to the refrigerator and took out a can of soda. "So tomorrow morning at 8:00 I'll get her. You want to come?"

I laughed. "Of course I do. She's my mother."

So I made up her bedroom, put flowers in it, put some Christmas decorations on the dresser, and counted the hours until morning. I called some of her friends and relatives to tell them the news. They were happy, but worried. I told them that if she did all right on Christmas Eve and on Christmas day some of them could come and see her after that. They understood, and hoped they would be able to come.

So mother came home on the morning of Christmas Eve. She sat in the car, so frail, so still, but when I peeped around at her from the back seat I saw that she was smiling. We helped her very slowly into the house and sat her in her favorite chair in our living room.

"Mom, sit here, enjoy the tree, I'll bring you a cup of tea or whatever you would like to have."

She smiled her wan little smile. "Thank you dear. Tea would be fine. I'm just going to sit here and look at everything. I tried to remember it while I was in the hospital, but sometimes you can't remember every little thing."

Rick came in with our dog, which had been penned in the backyard. The dog was so ecstatic to see mom that he could hardly be restrained, and Rick had to hold his collar and force him to quiet down. Mom loves the dog. "Hello Ralphie," she said, and held out her hand beside her chair.

Carefully my husband let the dog edge closer and he began joyously to lick her hand. She smiled and we all laughed. That evening with mom safely tucked into her bed and the house quieted for the night, Rick and I and Ralphie went out to the back patio, my husband and I to savor the night, and Ralphie to dash madly around the shrubbery.

I looked up at the starry night sky, and said, "What a beautiful night." Rick looked up too. "Santa must be up there somewhere by now."

So mom came home for Christmas, wan and frail. We're happy and we know she's happy. We're frightened and we know she's frightened.

But tomorrow will be Christmas day.

Christmas At The Newspaper

It was called the graveyard shift. It began at 11:00 p.m., after the final editions of the morning paper had gone to press.

So all of the great army of reporters, rewrite men, copy editors, photographers, and the principal editors of local and national news had all ended their shifts at 11:00 and gone home.

Normally, the graveyard shift would have had a few more people, although a skeleton crew compared to the regular night shift. The skeleton crew would have been there to pick up on urgent events which happened in the small hours of the morning, and to have news or information ready for the day shift when it arrived the next morning. But this was Christmas Eve.

And on holiday nights, the shifts were cut back to the absolute minimum, so that as many employees as possible could be home on this shift on Christmas night and New Year's Eve. So tonight at 11:00, when the graveyard shift began, Al was quite alone in the cavernous newsroom. As one of the younger members of the staff, his lack of seniority qualified him for the least desirable assignments. Being alone on Christmas night in the empty newspaper office was surely one of these.

After sitting in one of the chairs surrounding the big city desk and staring at the quiet telephones, he arose, stretched, and walked back toward the teletype room.

Here, normally, multiple machines would be spitting out long trails of paper with news stories from all over the world. After 11:00 p.m., many of them normally became silent but several would continue to function. Tonight, one lone machine was issuing paper from its printer. Al walked over to look at what was being printed. "Silent Night, Lonely Night," the machine typed. "What seems to many of us a festive occasion is often a tragic time for a surprising number of people who are alone and depressed. The seeming festiveness of the season for others can add to gloom and depression for those who are not a part of it. A noted psychiatrist says, . . ."

There was more, but Al turned away, suddenly with a sinking feeling inside. He left the teletype room and went on to what, in the old newspaper days, had been called the morgue. Now in more enlightened times it was called the library. He

138

stood looking at the rows of shelves and file cabinets and at the drawers filled with tapes and rolls of microfilm.

Here the silence and gloom seemed to be more overpowering. Here were the ghosts of news items now passé and famous people no longer famous. Still their records were held, in case someone ever needed to refer to them again.

He walked back toward the sports department, where there was a coffee machine. As he put coins in the machine and watched a cup drop, he looked at the teletype machines in the sports office. Sports had its own machines, and they would normally be constantly chattering, giving results and scores and items about sports stars and personalities. But tonight, they too were silent. He took the cup and began walking back toward the city desk.

Putting the cup down on the desk, he still could not bring himself to sit. So he walked to the tall windows overlooking the city street. Snow was falling, and already an inch or two covered the sidewalks.

"God, Susan." He rubbed his hand across his forehead still staring into the dark. "I miss you so damn much. How could I let you get away from me."

He turned and looked back toward the city desk where his coffee was steaming. He shook his head. "No, face it, dummy. You didn't let her get away. You acted like such a stupid twenty-two-year-old jerk that you ran her away." He watched the coffee steam.

One of the phones rang at the city desk. Reluctantly he moved to it and picked up the receiver. "City desk."

A quavering female voice was on the line. "My cat is missing," the voice said. "Did you hear me? My cat is missing."

Al drew a deep breath. "Lady, your cat is probably in some warm place and is probably okay. But the fact that your cat is missing is not news. If you want help, you should call the animal rescue league, but they are not going to come at midnight on Christmas night."

There was silence on the line. Finally the voice said, "Animal rescue league?" "Yes, but they are not going to come on Christmas night."

"What's their number?"

Al looked at the phone. "It's in the phone book, madam. In the white pages, under A. I'm sorry that your cat is not news." He hung up the phone and stared at it, his hands still on the receiver.

At last he picked up his coffee and sipped it. It was still too hot. "Damn," he said, and sat it down again.

Reluctantly, he looked at his watch. "Only 12:30. Six and a half hours to go. And then what? And then no Susan."

He sank dejectedly into a swivel chair, picked up the coffee again, burned his lip again. "Damn."

He looked at his watch again. Still 12:30. "All right, Al. Are you going to do something stupid? I mean are you going to do something *else* stupid?"

He put his hand on the phone again, took it off, put it back. "What possible good could it do to try to call her? Especially at an hour and a time like this? It can only make it worse. Why do it?"

He picked up the phone and began to dial. "She must be at her mother's. They've probably gone to bed. She can't be out somewhere. She must be there." He finished dialing. "But she's probably gone to bed."

He heard the rings begin as he held the phone to his ear. They sounded hollow, seemed to have an echo, seemed to be hurling themselves out, thin and frail across the dark snowy city.

Two rings. Three. Four. Five. "Oh God. She's not home. Or she's asleep. If I make her get up, she'll hate me."

Six rings. Seven. He hung up the phone with a slam. "What a stupid thing to do."

Across the city, in a big dark house, Christmas tree lights twinkled on and off in a corner of the darkness. Susan, breathless from having run down the stairs, snatched up the phone and put the receiver to her ear. The dull hollow hum of a dial tone was all that she heard. She held the phone for a few seconds, listening to the tone. Slowly she set it back down into its cradle.

"It had to be Al. Who else would possibly call at a time like this? Who else could be so stupid?"

She wrapped her dressing gown more tightly around her, hugging herself in the cold. "Al, you stupid loveable jerk. Why couldn't you just let it ring another once or twice? How could we have ever gotten into a situation like this?"

A voice floated through her ears from the stairwell. "Who was that, dear? Was someone on the phone?"

She turned back toward the stairs, her face alternately bright and dark in the flickering Christmas lights. "Just a wrong number, mother."

Al made another tour of the cavernous echoing room. To the teletypes. To the library. He still thought of it as the morgue. To the coffee machine, then remembered he still had his cup back at the city desk. He went back to the tall windows and looked into the street.

The carolers who had gone to the midnight service were returning. Walking slowly, leaving long scuff marks in the snow, they sang.

As they passed under the street light, their voices floated up to Al. "God rest ye merry gentlemen. Let nothing you dismay. Remember Christ our Savior is born on Christmas Day."

When they passed the street light, it was as if they were gone, disappeared into the dark. Al still stood at the window, watching as the snow fell slowly filling the scuffed footprint marks.

It's So Real

Jack and Sally decided to buy an artificial tree. All of their married lives, they had had a live tree every Christmas, first for themselves, then for the children.

But now the children were grown and away. And now they lived in a highrise condominium. And there was no longer the same appeal in thinking of finding a real tree, dragging it in, hauling it up on the elevator, going through all the effort, and then hauling it away again.

"Jack," Sally said, "You know I didn't use to like artificial trees because they looked just artificial. But they keep making them better. Have you noticed that?"

Jack had nodded. "Yes, I have. As a matter of fact, this year they have some that just look so real you really can't tell the difference. Maybe they even look better then real."

"I saw one at the store today," Sally said. "It really did look wonderful. I couldn't tell they were artificial until I saw one in a box. The display ones looked just like the real thing."

Jack walked around the living room, thinking of where a tree would best be placed. "Those realistic ones are pretty expensive, though, Sally." He looked up at his wife. "Do you think we want to spend that much?"

Sally was also looking around the room. "Well, Jack. Look at it this way. Say it costs $150. And if we spend $20 or $25 for a live tree each year, and we keep this good artificial one at least 6 or 7 years, we haven't really spent any more."

Jack paused by the sliding doors leading to the terrace. "That's a rationalization for you. But, in a way you're right. The added benefit is, we don't have to go out looking every year. We've got it. Stick it in the store room, then next year pull it out, put it together again and we don't have to worry." He looked at his wife and smiled. "So I guess we get one."

When the tree arrived and was put together and its carton stuck away in the store room, Jack and Sally admired it. They invited neighbors in to see it. "Doesn't it look real." Was the same expression from everyone who saw it. "It really does look just so real."

Eventually, Jack and Sally grew a little tired of hearing these expressions but still, they were proud of their tree. When it was decorated, it was a real work of art in the corner of their living room.

So the kids came to visit, commented on how real the tree looked, friends came and paid their respects to the tree, and the Christmas season swept by.

And after all the events of the season were over, Sally undressed the tree, putting the decorations away, while Jack was at work. The branches were really easy to remove from the sockets in the trunk and the entire thing, trunk, branches and all, slid so easily into the carton. Just a few tips of branches stuck out of the open end of the box, and she left it in the hallway for Jack to return to the storage room.

When Sally came home from shopping, the maid was fixing dinner. "Oh thanks, Ethel," Sally said. "It sure is good to have someone else fix dinner twice a week. That way I don't have to rush home on Tuesdays and Fridays."

"Glad to help out, Miss Sally," Ethel the maid said. "Mr. Jack should be home soon. Dinner won't be long."

When Jack came in, he kissed Sally and said hello to Ethel. "Smells good in there, Ethel. You're doing your usual fine job."

Looking around the living room, Jack said, "Gosh, Sally! I'd have helped you take the tree down. You didn't need to do that all by yourself. But thanks."

Sally smiled and said, "It was easy to take apart." She looked toward the hallway. "And easy to put in the box."

Jack also looked toward the hallway. "Where is the box? Don't tell me you lugged that down to the storage room by yourself?"

"Well, I don't see it. I had it leaning in the hall there."

Jack walked to the kitchen where Ethel was stirring something in a pot. "Ethel," he said, "did you see anything of that box with a tree in it?"

Ethel looked up from her stirring. "Yes Mr. Jack. I took it out."

"You lugged that all the way down to the storage room all by yourself. You didn't need to do that."

Ethel looked up, still stirring, still smiling. "Well I was taking the other trash out anyway. It didn't seem that heavy. So I was glad to do it."

Jack stared at her, in incredulity on his face. From behind him he heard a gasp from Sally. "You mean you threw it in the trash? Is that what you're telling me? You threw it away?"

Ethel nodded, glancing again at the pot. "That's what everybody does in these condos, Mr. Jack. When their tree is through, they just throw it in the trash. And the trashmen take them. That's how they do it."

Jack stared at her. Finally he said, "But it was in the box. It was in the box."

"But the tips was sticking out, Mr. Jack. That's how I knew it was the tree. I don't know why Ms. Sally had to cut it up like that. Nobody else does. They just throw them out whole."

Sally's voice came from behind Jack's back. "Oh my God."

Jack drew a deep breath. "Ethel, it was an artificial tree. You take it apart and put it in the box and then you keep it in the storeroom so you can put it up again the next year. It was an artificial tree."

Surprise and a look of anguish swept across Ethel's face. "Oh Mr. Jack, Ms. Sally, that's awful. And the trashmen already came. I just barely got it out there when they was backing their truck in." She laid down the spoon and wiped her hands on her apron, the look of anguish still on her face. She stared at Jack and Sally.

"But it looked so real. Them tips looked real, Mr. Jack." She turned her gaze imploringly at Sally. "It just looked so real."

The Snowstorm

They were driving up the New Jersey turnpike from Philadelphia. Carmella, in the passenger's seat looked at Alfredo, dark and handsome, behind the wheel.

From under her long dark lashes, her look became coy. "Do you feel like you've been married two years, Fredo?"

He laughed, and in his resonant baritone, said, "It feels like fifty." He saw the dubious look cross her face, and laughed again. "I want to have fifty more fifty years like these."

She smiled and laid her hand on his knee. "We will, my love." She looked ahead at the highway, then said, "I'm so glad we're going to see your parents for Christmas. We don't see them enough."

He looked at her. "I know you miss your mom and dad now that they are gone. And I know my mom and dad want you to feel that they are yours too." He put his hand over hers and squeezed it and she squeezed back, returning the pressure.

Turning to look into the back seat, Carmella said, "Such a bunch of gifts! They'll think we're crazy to bring so many."

Alfredo laughed. 'They always like lots of gifts. That's the way we do things." She sat back and smiled. "I'm beginning to feel the Christmas spirit. Maybe we should sing some carols."

"Or recite," he said. "'Twas two days before Christmas, and all through the car, not a creature was stirring . . ."

"Except Carm and Fredo!" she laughed.

Snow had begun to fall, the flakes whipped against the windshield by the speed of the car. Within only a minute or two, it seemed much thicker.

"I'm dreaming of a white Christmas," sang Carmella. Alfredo laughed. "It's beginning to look a lot like Christmas," he sang in return.

She launched into "Jingle Bells," then said, "Can you see all right? It sure seems to be getting thick."

"I can still see," Alfredo said. After a momentary silence, he added, "I was a little worried about my brother Manny being alone in the bakery. But if it's snowing like this in Philly, there won't be much business anyway."

Carmella nodded thoughtfully. "I wonder how far ahead or behind it is snowing. If it keeps on like this, it may be a real storm."

Alfredo peered ahead, watching the road from between swipes of the windshield wipers. "Just that quick there's a couple of inches on the road. It's because it's plenty cold enough to stick."

She also studied the road. "How many miles to Connecticut now?"

He looked at the odometer, doing a quick calculation. "Must be about a hundred to momma and papa's."

They both sat silently peering ahead into the snow. Carmella sang, trying to sound cheerful, "You better watch out, you better not pout. Santa Claus is coming . . ." "To town!" They both sang together, and laughed.

The snow continued to whip its flakes into the windshield, and the accumulation seems to be three to four inches already. Trying not to sound worried, Carm looked at her husband. "I don't know if we will make it today, Fredo. Maybe you should try to find a weather report on the radio." As she turned the radio knob, she added, "Maybe we should think about getting a motel. A lot of people may stop, and we might not get one if we wait too late."

Alfredo looked at her, a mock leer on his face. "You want to shack up with me, is that what you're telling me, woman?"

She laughed. "I do that all the time, buster." She looked at him teasingly, "And it's always with you."

Alfredo cut his laugh short as a voice from the radio began giving weather information. "Heavy accumulation from New Jersey north through New England. Travel warnings. Dangerous to travel without chains. Travelers are advised to postpone their trips unless travel is absolutely essential."

He turned the radio down and they looked at each other. "Sometimes they make it sound worse then it is," he said.

She looked back at the white road ahead, almost invisible through the whirling flakes. "Let's get a motel now, Fredo. We'll call your mom and dad from there, and tell them we'll see them tomorrow instead of today. Please Fredo?"

He studied her worried look for a moment, then nodded. "I'll watch for the next exit. I think we must be coming up on New Brunswick. I think that's exit 9."

Together they peered through the flying snow to try not to miss the green exit sign when it would appear. They had almost passed it when it became visible, even though they had slowed to 40 miles per hour and other traffic was moving at similar slower speeds. "That's it! It's right here!" Carmella called excitedly. "Don't miss it. Slow down!"

Alfredo was slowing down, but he laughed and said, 'The backseat is full of Christmas presents, so you have to do your backseat driving from where you are. But thanks, hon. I might not have seen it."

He guided the car very carefully down the exit ramp. Any false move or quick application of the brakes could send them into a skid and into a ditch. He worried that he wouldn't be able to slow sufficiently at the bottom of the ramp, but he managed to negotiate the left turn toward New Brunswick. Together they watched for a motel.

A lighted sign giving the name of a chain motel appeared on their right, almost magically becoming visible through the flying snow. "Okay, here's one," Carmella said, and Alfredo slowed the car even more. He had to guess as to where the entrance was, since everything was covered with snow, and he bumped two of the wheels over a curb as they slid to a stop under the entrance canopy.

"You sit tight, Carm, and I'll run in. Damn, I wish I had snow shoes." He laughed, trying to keep his young wife's spirits up.

In the motel office, the elderly clerk handed him a registration card and said, "Lucky you got here now. Only two rooms left. A lot of people are going to be in trouble."

Alfredo nodded, completing the form. Armed with the room key, he stepped back into the snow and waded through it to the car.

"Clerk says we're lucky," he reported to Carmella. "We got one of the last two rooms. It's upstairs on the second level. We'll have to make the best of it." She nodded. "I'm just glad we're here."

The room was standard highway motel style. Same furniture, same Naugahyde chair, same bedside table that they might see anywhere. Carmella looked around and said, dropping her suitcase, "At least we brought clothes and toilet stuff with us, since we were going to stay with mom and pop."

Alfredo sat on the bed and picked up the phone to call his parents in Connecticut. After a few moments, he spoke into the mouthpiece. "Mom! It's Fredo. How you doing?" He listened for a moment, then asked, "Is it snowing up there? It is huh?

Boy down here in New Jersey too." He listened again, then said, "Well mom, tell pop not to worry. We're not going to get there today because it's too dangerous. But we're in a motel and we're safe here in New Brunswick. Tomorrow when it clears up we'll come on up and be there on Christmas Eve instead of today." He listened again. "Love you too mom. Carm says hello."

He hung up the phone and looked back at Carmella. She was looking through parted draperies into the parking lot. "Keeps getting deeper. Sure glad we're here."

After dinner in the motel dining room, they turned up the heat in their room and watched television until Carmella reached above Alfredo's head and turned off the light.

She snuggled against him, nuzzling his neck. "Well, mister man. We have this motel room. I guess we're suppose to use it."

When Alfredo felt a beam of sunlight on his face he blinked his eyes open. The sunlight came through the gap in the draperies where Carmella stood in her nightdress, peering out.

"What's it look like, hon?" He asked.

She turned back with a strange look on her face. "Fredo, you won't believe this unless you see it. But our car has disappeared!"

Alfredo sat up. "You mean it's gone?"

She shook her head, her dark curls swirling around her shoulders. "No. I mean the snow is so deep that you can't see where the cars are."

154

He jumped up from the bed and hurried to join her at the window. Sure enough, snow had drifted so deep that it had covered all the cars on their side of the motel, making a smooth long deep drift without even the configuration of cars interrupting its smoothness.

"Gosh!" He continued to stare down. "Even though it's not snowing now, if the highway's like that, we can't leave. I guess we better check the news."

The news said that three feet of snow had fallen during the previous day and night, drifting in many places to four, five or more feet, that all highways were impassable, even the major interstates, and that it might be days before they could be cleared. Everyone was admonished to stay put and remain in a safe place.

Alfredo called his parents again. They too were snowed in, but had plenty of food, and weren't worried about themselves. They were worried about Alfredo and Carmella, but he assured them that they were safe and warm. "But," he said, "I know we won't get there today. I don't know about tomorrow. We may have to postpone Christmas." He laughed, then said, "Just joking, pop. But we'll have ours when we get there."

That day, there was nothing to do but eat the boring food in the restaurant, watch television, and make love. There were no newspapers. There were no deliveries to the motel. There was no traffic moving anywhere, because every road was completely impassable.

Christmas morning dawned bright and clear, but when Alfredo went to the window, the snow had not even begun to melt, and the streets he could see were still not cleared. He turned on the television, seeking a newscast. Again the report was that street clearing was almost at a standstill because of the enormity of the problem and the difficulty of getting full crews because of the Christmas holiday.

"Let's get breakfast while they still have some, hon," he said, extending his hands to lift Carmella from the bed.

In the restaurant, the waitress, who, like all the other kitchen and dining room staff, had been stuck at the motel, told them, 'The only thing we can make for breakfast is plain eggs or french toast made with pumpernickel bread." She laughed. 'That's the only bread we have left."

Fredo looked at Carmella across the booth and laughed. "I wonder what the other customers will think of that!" He looked again at the waitress and said, "We'll take it while you still got it."

Back in their room, she sat on the bed and he seated himself beside her. He put his arm around her shoulders. "Well, wife. Merry Christmas in a strange place!" He looked toward the window. "We can't even get at our Christmas presents. I thought I had something kind of neat that you'd like." He laughed. "We'll have to find out later."

She reached up to squeeze his hand where it lay on her shoulder. "And you can't see mine either. So you won't know it's a necktie until tomorrow." She laughed.

He joined in the laughter and gently laid her back on the bed. Kissing her cheek, then her lips, he said, "Well, darling, if we can stand each other after being forced into each other's company this way, maybe our marriage will be a long one."

She returned his kiss and looked into his eyes. "Fredo," she said, "Christmas for me is where you are. Merry Christmas."

Christmas Remembered

The gift-opening was finished, and Timmy's mother had gone to the kitchen, his father had taken the dog for a walk, and teenage Timmy and his friend Ralph, who had come to view the presents, were left alone in the family room with Timmy's grandpa, visiting for Christmas.

Timmy and Ralph tired of looking again at Timmy's gifts, and, almost as one, they pivoted on the carpet to face the old man sitting in the easy chair.

"Grandpa," Timmy said. "Ralph and I like to hear war stories from your time in the army." Ralph nodded in agreement. "Tell us one now, Grandpa. Please?"

Timmy's grandfather stared at them, smiling. His false teeth sparkled in the light from the Christmas tree.

Finally he folded his hands together and nodded. "Well, I'll tell you one. But since it's Christmas, I'll tell you a Christmas one."

His eyes stared into the darkest corner of the room. He was remembering. "This is about Christmas, and it's about the war. But it ain't about fighting. It's about something else that happened."

He rubbed the spotted back of one of his hands with the finger of the other, watching himself doing it. "A bunch of us got sick. Real sick. It was like a kind of flu, but I think they called it viral pneumonia. But it made us awful sick."

"Did you go to the hospital, Grandpa?" Timmy asked.

"Yes, we all had to go to the hospital. And we all were so sick that, in one way, we were glad to go and hope we could be helped to feel better." He paused a moment. "But the bad side was that it was right before Christmas when we went, and we were so sick we knew we had to stay through Christmas. Ain't that a way to spend Christmas? In the army hospital?"

Ralph frowned, nodding. "Sure don't sound too good."

Grandpa focused his eyes on Ralph. "But just being sick, having a fever, having a headache, having all the other bad stuff like throwing up, that still wasn't the worst of it to me. Not being able to be home at Christmas, that was bad too. But the worst, I think, was all those other guys, a whole ward full of them, maybe twenty or thirty."

Timmy looked up. "All those other guys what, Grandpa?"

Grandpa shifted his eyes to his grandson. "All those other guys coughing. Coughing." He emphasized the word putting a hollow sound to it. "Coughing all day. Coughing all night. And you never knew when the next cough would come. But you knew it would be soon. And one would wake the others up and they'd all start in like a symphony orchestra."

Ralph and Timmy laughed. "How do you mean that, Grandpa?"

He smiled grimly. "I mean that when twenty or thirty of them all got going together, it was like twenty or thirty different instruments. Some of them had deep coughs sounded like bassoons. Some of them had medium coughs sounded maybe like baritone horns or something. Some of them had high hacking coughs I don't know what they sounded like. Maybe they sounded like marimbas."

The boys laughed again. Their imaginations had been stirred.

"But," Grandpa continued, "it was awful. Head hurt. Stomach hurt. Fever. And can't sleep. Because of the dadratted coughing serenade." The boys laughed again.

"But, you had to do it. You had to take your medicine. You had to let the nurses come and take your temperature, and feel your pulse, and do other stuff to you sometimes."

"What other stuff, Grandpa?" Timmy asked, a mischievous sparkle in his eyes.

"Never mind what other stuff. They do stuff to you in the hospital." He paused a moment. "But all of that aside, cough,

161

cough, cough, Christmas day came. Here it was Christmas, and we were still in the blankety blank hospital."

Ralph turned his head to look at Timmy's tree. "Did they have a Christmas tree in the hospital?"

Grandpa nodded. "Yes, they had a little one back in the corner with some tinsel hung on it. We didn't care about that. We just wished we were home seeing friendly faces. And all the nurses would do us was stick us with needles and stuff like that."

He looked at the boys who were still listening rapidly. "But, something good happened. We couldn't go home, we couldn't get out of the hospital. But something good happened on Christmas day and I remember it still."

"What was that Grandpa?" both boys said almost simultaneously.

"Well these ladies came in. They were called gray ladies. They had something to do with the Red Cross. But you know what they brought? They brought Christmas presents, by golly! Christmas presents!"

Ralph and Timmy both grinned. "Neat!" Ralph said.

"And this nice Gray Lady, she was probably some middle-aged mother of some other soldier, she comes up to my bed and she takes my hand, and she says, 'We're so sorry you're here, soldier. We know you'd like to be home for Christmas.' And other Gray Ladies were at other soldiers' beds."

"So what happened?" Timmy demanded.

Grandpa smiled at them. "First she gives me an orange. Bright orange orange. It looked like something wonderful to me

there in the hospital. Because somebody was thinking of me."
He looked into the faces of his two listeners, 'And then she gives
me this wrapped-up present. She says, 'Here's another gift for
you from us. We wish it could be more. We hope it's something
you'll like and use.' Then she squeezed in my hand again, and
says, 'Merry Christmas!" Grandpa sat quietly looking at the
boys. They looked back at him.

Finally Ralph broke the silence. "So what was it? What did
she give you? What was the present?"

"Yeh, what?" Timmy chimed in.

"Well, I unwrapped it. While she was still standing there.
And it was a kind of a leather toilet article kit. It wasn't made out
of real leather because this was the war. But it had a zipper and
inside it had a soap dish with a top to it and it had a toothbrush
holder." His eyes lifted again to the far wall, remembering.
"So I says to her, thanks ever so much, missus. This is really
something I can use. And Merry Christmas to you!"

He looked again at the boys, his eyebrows raised. "And you
know what, boys? I still got that toilet article kit today! All
these years!" He looked at them, his eyes fixing theirs. "You
want to see it?"

He raised himself laboriously from the chair, pushing himself
slowly erect and, making sure of his balance, turned toward his
bedroom. "I'll show it to you."

The boys looked at each other. Timmy winked at Ralph.
"Yes, sure, Grandpa. We want to see it."

Mistletoe

She had come in early to hang the mistletoe. She had stood on a chair and fastened it with a thumbtack to the top of the door frame which delineated the entrance to her work area from that of her boss.

She had wanted it to be up before he came in. This was the last day of scheduled work before the company took a long holiday. She wouldn't admit to herself why she had wanted to do this, or what outcome she anticipated.

In the months before now, she had vacillated between feeling that her boss was interested in her in a personal way, and feeling that he was just a very polite, nice guy. On days when she felt convinced it was the latter, she was not nearly as excited about her job. On days when she leaned toward the former hypothesis, her heart fluttered frequently at sight of him, and sometimes her palms grew moist.

Now, when she saw him enter from the hallway, it was heart flutter and moist palm time. She had worn her best dress that could be considered suitable for the office.

"Good morning, Julie!" he said in his warm strong voice. "How are you today?"

She smiled what she hoped was her best smile, and hoped her eyes were sparkling. "Good morning, Bob," she said. Months earlier, when they had begun working together, he had told her that, in private, they should be on a first name basis.

Carrying his briefcase, he went through the connecting door into his own office. He seemed not to have noticed the mistletoe. She sat, fingering papers on her desk, thinking she should get to work.

Suddenly he was back standing by her desk. "I brought a gift for you, Julie. I never know what to get." He looked awkward as he held out a small box. "I hope you like it."

She took it, letting her fingers touch his as she moved the box from his hand to hers. She put it on the top of her desk blotter, and said, "Thank you. Whatever it is." She looked up and smiled again. "I got you one too."

She opened the drawer of her desk and rummaged for a moment, and then pulled out a package wrapped in Christmas paper. "I never know either. So I hope you won't think it's something dumb." She handed it to him, her fingers touching his again.

"Of course it's not dumb." He looked at the small box. "Whatever it is. It's heavy whatever it is."

She laughed. "Just don't hit me with it." Then she looked at the package on her blotter, and back up at him. "Shall we open them?"

He smiled and sat in the chair beside her desk. "Sure. Let's do."

He began to take the ribbon and wrapping from the package he held, and she loosened the ribbon and pulled tape loose from the package on her desk. His was opened first.

"Well!" He said enthusiastically. "No wonder it's heavy. It's a paperweight with my college crest on it." He looked up at her smiling. "How did you know how to get one of those?"

She laughed. "I sneaked a look at one of your college bulletins when it came in. I hope you'll forgive me."

He laughed. "If you hadn't, I wouldn't have this. Of course I forgive you. Nothing to forgive. You're my secretary. If you can't look at it, who can?"

She had her eyes lowered to the box which was now revealed beneath the wrappings on her desk. She lifted the lid and stared at the small necklace lying in cotton. She looked up, her eyes misting. "It's gorgeous. You shouldn't have given me a thing like that." She saw the consternation on his face, so she added warmly, "But I love it! It's very, very nice. I just feel bad." She shook her head, her auburn hair flying. "No I don't mean that either. I feel good. I'm not sure that you should give me something so - personal."

He laughed. "The more you say, the more you dig a hole for yourself. Just if you like it, wear it. If you don't, I'll take it back."

She snatched up the box and held it against her chest. "I love it. I love it. I won't let you take it back. Thank you so much." She rose quickly from her chair, leaned over and kissed him on the cheek, then sat back quickly.

He looked at her. She thought his expression was strange and she wondered what to make of it. He rose from his chair.

"It's the last day of work before Christmas, and we're thanking each other for our gifts. So I get to kiss you too." He moved around toward where she was sitting. She followed him with her eyes.

"Yes," she said in a stifled voice. "I guess you do."

From behind her chair, he bent over as she raised her face toward him, and kissed her warmly, gently on the lips, then raised back to continue standing behind her. She felt the color rising in her face. She felt her heart pounding.

"Well," he said in a strange soft tone. "I've got to get out of here. You know I'm catching a plane to my folks for the holiday." He took her hand. "I hope you have a good one. I hope I'll see you when I get back." Her hand felt small and hot in his. She looked up and tried to smile without losing control.

"Yes. Merry Christmas to you and your family." She paused. "And I'll see you when you get back."

He hastened into his office, packed a few additional things in his briefcase, set his new paperweight on his desk - proudly she thought - and then hurried for the door waving goodbye. "I'll miss the plane." He laughed. "If I do, I'll come back."

And he was gone. She sat there, her mind a combination of blank space and turmoil. The other door opened again.

She looked up. One of the salesman had come in and was walking toward her. Suddenly he stopped. "Hey look at that!" said enthusiastically. "Mistletoe!" He turned to her. "Come on then, gal." He held out his hands.

She laughed ruefully, and rose from her chair, walking reluctantly to clasp his extended hands. He led her to the doorway under the mistletoe and planted a robust kiss on her cheek. "If I knew you better, I'd take more advantage of this," he said.

She laughed. "Lucky you don't." She backed away. "Merry Christmas, Mr. Glover."

"Boss is gone already?" he asked.

She nodded, sitting back at her desk. "Had to catch a plane."

"Okay. I'll be going then. Merry Christmas! Merry Mistletoe!" He laughed, closing the door behind him.

She took a deep breath, her fingers touching the box which contained her necklace, remembering the feel of her boss' lips on hers.

"And the irony is," she told herself, "he never even saw the mistletoe. And we didn't even need it."

The Bell Ringers

Each year, Roger and Pearl would volunteer several hours of their time to ring bells for the Salvation Army. Their kettle was placed near the entrance of the department store in the local shopping center.

At their advanced age, each knew that the feet would suffer, the joints would stiffen, and the muscles would cry out following their hours of volunteer duty. But, in the spirit of the Christmas season, they kept coming back.

So, on this day, as usual, they danced to the cadence of their bell ringing or rang the bells to the cadence of their somewhat stiff leg motions. "Merry Christmas!" They would call to the potential shoppers entering the store, and to the bundle-bearing buyers as they left.

Some shoppers would smile and tuck a dollar into the slot in the bucket. Others would fish in their purses for fifty cents or a quarter, children would beg their mothers for a few cents to have the pleasure of putting it in the pot.

"Merry Christmas!" Roger and Pearl would call after each donation. "And a Happy New Year!"

Today they collected a couple of young toughs as hecklers. Dressed in the outrageous garb which showed a flouting of authority, the teenage boys sat on a nearby wall and called out taunts to Roger and Pearl.

"That bell ringing sure is a pain. You're hurting our ears!"

The other boy laughed, and said, "And that dancing. You call that dancing? Looks like you've got the staggers!"

At first Roger and Pearl ignored them, continuing to ring the bell and do dance steps for the passers by, who continued to insert dollars and coins into the slot and to be rewarded with cries of "Merry Christmas, Happy New Year!" from the pair of bell ringers.

When children would beg their mothers for change and put it in the pot, the boys on the wall would call out, "That kid's too dumb to know what she's doing!"

Or, one of the taunters would say, "That looks like about seven cents that kid put in. Salvation Army will never survive that way!"

Still Roger and Pearl continued their efforts. During a brief lull, while they continued to ring their bells, one of the boys called out, "I said that bell ringing hurts my ears. Isn't there any way to stop it?"

"Yeh," the other boy yelled. "It hurts my ears too. Why don't you cut it out?"

Pearl looked at them, still ringing, still dancing. "You can get me to stop for a dollar!" She laughed.

Roger joined in the laughter. Then he said, "Yeh, and you can get me to stop for another dollar!"

The boys were momentarily silent, then both shouted almost in unison. "It ain't worth it, man! This is chicken stuff! You won't catch us wasting money on that!"

Still shoppers flowed by, in and out of the store, and Roger and Pearl rang their bells. Smiles and happy responses were the normal order of the day, with only a sourpuss here and there. Still the boys sat, injecting an occasional heckling comment. Then a mother approached with a small boy who walked awkwardly. The boy looked at the bucket, at the bell ringers, and then up to his mother who held his hand. "Can I pay? Can I?"

His speech came out with difficulty, and, Roger, looking at him, surmised that perhaps he was a Down's syndrome child.

The mother hesitated, smiling apologetically at Roger and Pearl then delved into her purse.

"More small change!" Came the heckling call from the boys on the wall. The mother handed the child some coins, and he advanced awkwardly to the bucket and carefully, slowly, slid the coins through the slot. Then he looked up to Pearl. "Can I ring? Can I?" He asked eagerly.

Pearl laughed and extended the bell to him. Wrapping his fingers carefully around the handle, he made awkward jerking strokes, each of which caused the bell to clang. He laughed happily.

"Dumb kid!" came a catcall from the wall, seemingly ignored by the mother and the bell ringers.

Pearl took the bell back when the child handed it toward her and rang it herself. She said, "Now, young man." She leaned even closer. "Merry Christmas!" She paused looking expectantly at him. "Merry Christmas, and what?"

The boy looked at her then at his mother and back to Pearl again. Pearl said again, "Merry Christmas! Merry Christmas - and - what else?"

A smile spread across the youngsters face. In his awkward speech he shouted, "Merry Christmas - and - Happy Easter!"

Everyone laughed, and Pearl hugged the boy and smiled warmly at his mother. "What a wonderful young man!" She bent back to the youngster, "And Happy Easter to you!"

Mother and child entered the store. The boys on the wall were rolling with laughter. "Happy Easter!" They called out between peals of laughter. "Dumb kid! Happy Easter!"

Roger and Pearl studied them for a moment, then looked at each other. They resumed ringing their bells and shuffling into their dance steps. More shoppers approached, some with children, and each time a new shopper drew near, Pearl or Roger would call out while ringing the bell, "Merry Christmas! And Happy Easter!"

Many shoppers looked incredulously back at Roger and Pearl, then laughed.

Sometimes the shoppers would respond with "Merry Christmas!" And many of them would donate to the Salvation Army's bucket for the benefit of the poor. Occasionally, someone would respond with "And a Happy Easter to you, too!"

So Pearl and Roger danced and sang, using their new found greeting and warming the hearts of the parents and children streaming in and out. "Merry Christmas! And a Happy Easter!"

And, eventually, the young hecklers departed.

Getting To Pittsburgh

Snow was falling. Soft, light flakes, sparkling in the lights of Connecticut Avenue, making walking more hazardous as I rounded the corner.

Washington's downtown streets seemed bejeweled with colored lights for the Christmas season. People tightened their coat collars against the snow and moved more rapidly in the early dark of December.

I watched my feet, stepping carefully in the thickening snow, wishing I had my overshoes. So, when a voice seemed to speak to me, I looked up quickly, startled.

"Pardon me, sir," the voice said, gravelly, wheezing slightly. It belonged to a tall, emaciated man in an ancient army overcoat. His shaggy eyebrows were collecting snowflakes, turning whiter.

"I'm trying to get home to Pittsburgh for Christmas. I just need another dollar to have enough for bus fare."

His watery, bloodshot eyes looked at me, looked away, looked back again. "Could you help me out?"

We stood a foot apart, snowflakes falling between us. A few awkward seconds slid by before I opened a button of my coat to reach into my pants pocket.

I smiled as I extracted a dollar bill and held it out to him. "Everybody should be home at Christmas, if they can," I said.

His hand closed over the bill and disappeared instantly into the voluminous army coat. "Merry Christmas, sir," his wheezing voice said. "God bless you."

He moved in one direction and I in the other, toward the shop which had advertised an attractive last-minute gift idea.

When I emerged from the shop, flakes were still falling, people still hurried, and the snow was half an inch deeper.

Heading back toward the side street where I had parked my car, I was once again watching my steps to keep from slipping. Only now I had a package to hold under my coat, protecting it from the snow. Lights twinkled from lamp posts and shop windows.

A voice in my ear startled me, stopped me in my tracks.

"Pardon me, sir," the gravelly, wheezing voice said. I looked up to see the tall, emaciated man in his too-large army coat.

"I'm trying to get home to Pittsburgh for Christmas," he told me, his watery eyes, under snow-whitened brows, looking through me. "I just need another dollar for bus fare. Could you help me out?"

I watched his stubbled, lined face. No glimmer of recognition showed in his eyes. My immediate reaction was to tell him he had panhandled me already. I was tempted to embarrass him by telling him he should look at the people he approached.

Then I thought, "He's probably beyond embarrassment. He must be in some stage of desperation beyond my capacity to imagine." I knew now what I had tried not to acknowledge on his first approach - his seasonal pitch was a cover for collecting booze money.

His eyes looked away, back at me, away again. He was getting edgy, afraid I would turn him down. What, I wondered, could I say or do to change him on a snowy night on Connecticut Avenue?

Nothing, I decided. I opened my coat, found another dollar, held it out. "Everybody should be home at Christmas, if they can," I said.

The bill disappeared into the army coat. "Merry Christmas, sir. God bless you." He moved away.

I turned again in the direction of my car. Snowflakes struck gently against my face, melting in small wet kisses.

"Merry Christmas," I said softly, ironically, to myself, leaning into the drifting flakes. "I hope you find your Pittsburgh, wherever it is."

The Christmas Dinner

"You know," Marian said. "I'll bet there are lots of older people who don't do anything at Christmas - just stay home alone."

Her friend Laura set her teacup on the end table beside her. Marian and Laura were having their customary afternoon visit. "I think you're right, Marian. When you stop to think about it, you can just off the top of your head come up with a few, who have no kids, or whose wife is dying or whose husband is dead and you know they don't go away anywhere."

Marian smiled. "Not that we're spring chickens, Laura. And not that our husbands are still alive either." She sipped from her teacup. "But we have friends. Some of those others do too. But maybe some don't."

Laura nodded. "Even if you have friends, Christmas can be a pretty lonely time. I wonder if there's something we can do to help."

Marian smiled. "Why do you think I'm bringing this up?" Laura laughed, and Marian continued, "I was just thinking today, maybe we could be, not the whole committee, but the organizers to get a committee started. We could plan a dinner for anybody in our church who hasn't gone away and doesn't have other things to do on Christmas."

"We could have it in the church hall like we have other dinners at other times."

So they talked to the leaders of the congregation, they talked to the minister, they got a go-ahead to do the dinner this year on a trial basis, and, three Sundays before Christmas, they made announcements, posted a bulletin, and put out a sign-up sheet in the social hall for those who planned to attend.

At the end of that first Sunday, Marian was astonished to see that thirty-five people had put their names on the list. She and Laura stood looking at the names, and said, "Well, some of them aren't even old."

Laura looked at her friend. "So what? If they don't have any place to go, do we discriminate against the young?" She looked back at the list. "Besides, strange how you and I think fifty is young. Those fifty-year-olds probably think those forty-year-olds are young."

Marian laughed. "Of course. If they don't have any place to go, we'll make them welcome."

So the sign-up list grew to fifty. Marian and Laura were delighted to think they were going to provide a social activity that could involve so many people who might otherwise be alone. Others on the committee planned for the food, and a separate group planned entertainment.

And they resolved various questions. Should there be a gift exchange? Should there be carol singing? Should people pay to attend? They had tentatively settled on a small donation from each person, but then decided if the person would prefer to bring some bowl or platter of prepared food, they would not otherwise pay.

The dinner was to be at 2:00 p.m. on Christmas day. The committee was to arrive much earlier to be sure everything was done. When Laura and Marion arrived at noon, food preparers were already at work, but they immediately detected signs of panic among the committee members who had preceded them. "The furnace isn't running!" One of the preparers wailed. "We don't know who to call, we don't know anything about the furnace. It looks like disaster!"

Marion could see that several of the women were ready to throw up their hands and surrender. She looked at Laura. Laura said, "I know one of the retirees was a plumber. Maybe we could call him."

"Do plumbers know about furnaces?" Marion asked.

Laura shrugged. "If he doesn't, maybe he knows who does."

So Laura was delegated to try to. get emergency help, because the dining room would be at near freezing temperature without the furnace operating. Women in the kitchen were keeping warm by the stove.

Laura found someone who knew how to restart the furnace, which was all that the problem was, and the dining room gradually grew warmer. Forty people came, not fifty, so there was surplus food.

But those who came loved the social event, most of them like singing carols afterward, and, for those who stayed, there was Marian's mind-reading act which she had recalled from her high school days. Since no one in the church group had ever seen her do it, she was an enormous success.

Hours later, Laura and Marian still sat near the church kitchen. There were still loose ends of clean-up to deal with. "I don't think I was ever this tired on Christmas day, even when I had three kids at home and had to cook the dinner and do everything else besides."

Laura laughed. "You weren't this old, either." She looked around the room. "But I'd be lying if I didn't tell you I'd felt the same. I think we put more effort into this then we would have done for something at home."

They both sat staring out into the room. Then Laura turned to look at Marian. "But wasn't it worth it? Did you see those happy faces?"

Marian nodded. "I'll tell you what," she said thoughtfully. "After all these years, you're suppose to know it. But sometimes it seems to slip out of your mind or get out of focus." She looked back at her friend. "Doing something for others is the best kind of thing you can do."

When they had finished cleaning and turned off the lights, they walked together to the parking area. The neighborhood was bejeweled with Christmas lights. The sky was bejeweled with stars.

The Gifts Disappear

McGregor had noticed her while they were on the plane. Now, standing in the baggage delivery area, he mentally remarked on her elderly frailty. The teenage girl standing next to her must be her granddaughter.

The reason he noticed them now was the state of agitation which they demonstrated. The old lady groped for a seat at the side of the baggage area, as if she might faint. The teenager held her arm, as if to keep her from falling and they both appeared stricken.

It was not McGregor's practice to intrude on the privacy of others, but he saw no one else around who seemed to have any interest in the old lady, so he stepped toward where she was sitting. "Good afternoon ma'am." The girl looked up with an expression of fear on her face. "My name is McGregor. It appears that you are in some distress. Is there any way I can help?"

Still the teenager said nothing, staring at him, a slight frown on her face. But finally the old lady said in a quavering voice, "My shopping bag. It's not here." She looked around aimlessly. "I'm afraid someone has taken it."

His eyes searched the area which swarmed with people awaited their bags to be delivered on the carousel. "What was in the bag, ma'am?"

She looked up at him with pale grey eyes. "All our Christmas gifts that we were bringing. It's for my daughter and my son-in-law and my other grandchildren. All the gifts." Her voice trailed off to a sad softness. "All our gifts."

"And they were wrapped in Christmas paper?" He looked again around the room. "Yes. Christmas paper," the girl finally spoke in a sharp voice. "What do you think they would be wrapped in?"

The old lady put out her hand to touch the girl's arm. "Dear, the nice man is trying to help us. Please don't be like that."

The girl looked chastened. "I'm sorry," she said. "It's just that we're upset. What can we do?"

McGregor studied the room again. "Just stay right here for the moment. Please don't move. I'll need to find you when I get back." He started away, then looked back. "Please. Stay here." And he moved quickly away toward the escalator.

On the upper level, be found the office of the airport police, and inside a young man in uniform with a silver bar on each shoulder. When the man looked up from his desk, McGregor said, "Are you the person in charge?"

The officer frowned slightly. "I'm in charge of this shift. What's the trouble?" McGregor pointed to the floor. "An old lady downstairs at the baggage carousel had her shopping bag stolen. It was full of Christmas gifts."

The lieutenant was staring at McGregor's face. Slowly his eyebrows rose. "I know who you are. You're that magician fellow, right? I saw you on television." When McGregor didn't respond, the officer persisted. "That's you, am I right? McGregor? Right?"

McGregor nodded impatiently. "Yes, but we need to help this old lady. Can you get some officers on it right away?"

The officer looked at him coolly. "What's it to you? We can handle our own business here. Is the old lady with you?"

McGregor shook his head impatiently. "No she's a little old lady with a teenage girl. She has nobody to help her - unless you can help her. She can't run up and down the stairs. I'm trying to be a good samaritan."

Slowly the lieutenant nodded. "Yeh. Okay, sorry, I know you're trying to help. We get a little edgy around here this time of year."

Still he did not rise from his desk but looked toward the wall. Then he said, "Geez, the second one this afternoon. The second shopping bag."

McGregor raised his eyebrows. "You mean another shopping bag theft was reported this afternoon?"

The lieutenant nodded. "About an hour ago."

McGregor looked at him. "And for every one that's reported, there may be another one or more where the people just took their loss and walked off." He paused. "It may be an organized theft ring. They may be sweeping the place."

The lieutenant stood. "Or a couple of different creeps got tempted by a couple of different shopping bags." He stepped out from behind the desk. "Let me get a couple of men and see what kind of search we can run." He picked up a walkie talkie and started toward the door. "Probably hopeless, though."

Back in the baggage area, McGregor reported to the elderly lady and her granddaughter. "The security police are doing a search now. Please wait a little longer. We'll see if we can't find it for you."

The old lady smiled. "We're so grateful. Thank you."

The young girl smiled weakly, saying nothing.

"But don't get your hopes up. We're trying. We'll do the best we can. If you will excuse me for a few minutes now I'm going to watch some of what they do."

He watched the security police as they searched the restrooms, the employee locker rooms, the area behind the wall from which the baggage carousel emerged. He watched them interview the dispatcher at the cab stand outside the baggage area. He saw them interview skycaps who assist passengers with their baggage from the carousel to their cars or taxis, and he saw them interview clerks at the car rental counters which were nearby.

All to no avail.

"Nothing," the lieutenant told McGregor. "It's just like the one before."

McGregor stared off across the baggage area. Finally he said, "I'm willing to play a long shot to see if we can't catch the culprit here." He looked at the lieutenant. "Would you help me?"

The lieutenant narrowed his eyes. "You have no authority here."

"Only what you allow me, lieutenant," McGregor said, smiling. "I just have an idea that might possibly work. It will only work if you help. If we catch the guy, you'll be the one in charge of catching him. What can you lose?"

The lieutenant looked back at McGregor. "What's in it for you?"

"It's two days before Christmas. I'm on my way home. Like I said, if I feel like helping a little old lady, isn't this the season to do it?"

The lieutenant looked over to where the elderly lady and her teenage companion were still sitting. Slowly he nodded his head. "I guess so. Spirit of the season." He looked back at McGregor. "What is it you want to do?"

McGregor said, "Well, if there's a guy watching his chance to snatch Christmas gift bags, and if he hasn't got enough yet, then he's taking them someplace nearby and stashing them. He won't take another one, if he comes back, unless he thinks he's free from the eyes of the police." He smiled at the lieutenant.

191

"Therefore we have to create the illusion that there are no police."

The lieutenant looked back incredulously. "I've got to have men on duty. What are you talking about?"

McGregor swung his hand around the room. "I'm talking about for the next hour, letting me and somebody else who doesn't look like a cop keep our eyes open in the baggage area. Have you got somebody coming on duty who isn't in uniform yet?"

The lieutenant still appeared dubious. "I'm not authorized to let guys be in plain clothes around here. There are a couple of guys coming on duty, but I'm not authorized."

McGregor smiled and looked into his eyes. "But for a little old lady two days before Christmas, will you?"

The lieutenant met McGregor's eyes. Finally he said, "Yes. For an hour. Because it's Christmas."

McGregor went to the elderly lady and the girl, took the girl's hand and tucked a twenty dollar bill into it. "We're still going to try to pull something off here that might get your bag back. But we don't want you waiting down here. So why don't you take your grandmother up to the restaurant and have a meal or a snack, a piece of pie and some coffee, whatever. On me. And I'll find you up there later. Please wait for me."

The old lady raised her head. "You shouldn't be paying for us. You don't even know us. Why would you do that?"

McGregor smiled again. "It's the Christmas season, ma'am. I hope this is my good deed for today." He smiled at the girl. "Please take her upstairs. I'll find you soon."

So they left, and he and the security officer still in street clothes worked out a system, while the lieutenant kept all other police away from the baggage area. McGregor and the plain clothes men each had walkie talkies concealed inside their jackets. They took seats at each end of the baggage area and pretended to be watching for someone or waiting for baggage near the two carousels. They tried to look disinterested, to have a suitcase next to them, to be checking their watches, to be watching the T.V. monitor announcing arriving flights, all in the interest of seeming like tourists.

Minutes crept by. McGregor had studied so many faces and watched so many innocent people move baggage and shopping bags, that his eyes were growing tired. Suddenly the walkie talkie in his pocket crackled.

"I've got him spotted," the voice said from his speaker. "He's a small dark guy with a tan windbreaker. He grabbed a shopping bag full of Christmas gifts and zipped right out the door toward the parking building."

McGregor whipped his walkie talkie out and depressed the button to speak.

"Alert the other guys in the parking building," he said quickly. "And alert the lieutenant."

He met the other man by the taxi cab rank. 'The trick is to let him think we haven't seen him," McGregor said. "Otherwise he won't lead us to his car, if that's where he's stashing the stuff."

There were men concealed at each end of the parking building on orders of the lieutenant. Their direction was to watch for the man who had been described to them on their walkie talkie, and to keep an eye on him without revealing themselves until he had gotten to his car.

As the two of them walked into the parking building, McGregor heard a voice from the walkie talkie in his hand. "Got him spotted near his car." The voice said. "He's got his keys out."

"Okay, move in quick," he heard the lieutenant's voice say.

Later, McGregor led the older lady and the teenager to the security office. On the floor by the lieutenant's desk, there were six shopping bags filled with packages wrapped in Christmas paper.

"Do you recognize one of these, ma'am?" McGregor asked.

A look of astonishment was on the old woman's face as she saw so many shopping bags and so many gifts. But suddenly her eyes lighted. "That's it! That one on the back left there. The one with all the poinsettia paper!"

The granddaughter laughed. "You always liked to use poinsettia paper, Grandma." She looked at McGregor. "Where's the man who stole these?"

The lieutenant answered. "He's already on his way to jail. Lucky we caught him when we did. He said that was his last load that he was taking to the car when we got him" He smiled at them. "I guess his car was full."

They laughed, and, with the shopping bag safely in the hands of the teenager, they turned toward the door. The old lady turned back to McGregor.

"Sir, I don't even know your name, you've been so wonderfully gracious." She turned her head toward the lieutenant. "And you too officer."

They both smiled, and McGregor said, "I'm just a friend." He looked at the two of them, opening the door for them. "Merry Christmas."

Behind him he heard the lieutenant's voice. "Yes folks. Merry Christmas to you."

After Midnight

The boys sat at the dining room table, playing cards. The game was five hundred rummy. They played and drank Pepsi Cola from the bottle.

Jerry and George had come from their respective homes to join brothers Dick and Wally. It was Christmas Eve, and for some reason both Jerry's parents and George's parents had been willing, perhaps even relieved, to hear them say they had a place to go for a few hours.

Occasionally, one of the boys would laugh as he slapped down a card to take a trick. Occasionally, a boy would pour additional spanish peanuts into his twelve-ounce Pepsi bottle. Then, when he took a swig of Pepsi, he would get two or three peanuts along with it.

Occasionally too they would take turns singing the Pepsi commercial of that era, which they all seem to enjoy. "Nickel, nickel, nickel, trickle, trickle, trickle, trickle. Pepsi Cola hits the spot. Twelve full ounces that's a lot. Twice as much for a nickel too, Pepsi Cola is the drink for you. Nickel, nickel, nickel, nickel, trickle, trickle, trickle, trickle." And they would all laugh uproariously.

Pepsi in those days competed with Coke by selling a bottle twice as large for the same price as the wasp-waisted Coke bottle.

George sat back and surveyed the table. "Boy, I am glad I got the tree trimmed early. It sure is better being here playing cards then still having to be back there hanging tinsel."

"Me too," Jerry said, nodding. "We got ours up yesterday. My mom hates to do it on Christmas Eve. She thinks that's too late."

This seemed to trigger a thought for George. He looked around the dining room and through the archway into the living room. "Where's your tree, Dick? I suddenly realized I didn't see it anywhere."

"Yeah," Jerry chimed in. "Come to think of it. Where is your tree?"

Dick looked at his younger brother Wally and smiled. "We have a special method. We put up our tree later than anybody."

George looked around again. "Yeah, but where is it? Is it still outside?" Wally laughed. "Part of our special method is that we get our tree later than anybody. It isn't here yet."

He looked at his brother Dick and they smiled a secret smile.

"Gosh," Jerry said. "When do you get it?"

Dick looked at the clock on the wall. "After midnight. We still got three hours."

George's eyes widened in surprise. "After midnight?" He turned to look at the clock behind him. "I don't even know if we can stay that late. I thought maybe we could help you if you didn't have it up and trimmed yet."

Jerry looked uncomfortable. "I'm not sure I came over here to trim another tree."

Dick laughed. "Don't worry, don't worry. Wally and I can handle it." He gathered up the cards. "Okay, let's deal the next hand." Wally picked up his bottle and, prior to dropping more peanuts down its neck, serenaded the other three with another rendition of "Nickel, nickel, nickel, trickle, trickle, trickle ..."

An hour later, George looked again at the clock. "Maybe I could call my parents. I'd really like to stay and see how you do this special tree deal. I'll tell them it's something special that I need to help you guys with. It would be neat to stay here after midnight." He looked at Dick and Wally. "Would that be okay if they say yes?"

"Sure," Dick said, dealing cards. "You know where the phone is. It's in the hall. Hurry so we can play this hand."

In a few minutes George came back, grinning. "She said now that I'm fifteen, she guesses that I can do it." He looked at the others. "Probably a good thing my dad was out."

Jerry shifted uncomfortably. "After this game, maybe I'll run home and see if I can stay. It's not far, and I'd rather ask my mom face to face. Too easy for her to say no on the phone."

Wally looked at the others. "I thought maybe after this game we might want to play a little doubles ping-pong. I've got the stuff set up in the basement."

George took a swig of his Pepsi and peanuts. "Okay with me." Later, George and Wally volleyed the ping-pong ball back and forth across the net while Dick waited to play the winner. Jerry had gone home, as he had announced earlier, to negotiate with his mother.

George prepared to serve. "What's your mom doing, Wally? I haven't seen her all evening."

As Wally opened his mouth to answer, George drove the serve past him off the corner of the table and laughed. Wally frowned. "Dirty trick George. I thought you really wanted to know."

George laughed again, "I do, but that didn't stop me from serving."

Dick spoke from the sideline. "She's over helping one of the neighbors wrap packages. Mom always has hers wrapped by the middle of summer and they are hidden in an upstairs closet."

George looked at Dick in astonishment, both because his mother had performed such an amazing feat, and because Dick knew the location of the packages.

"Wow! I can't imagine anybody doing Christmas shopping in the summer Fantastic! Why does she do that?"

"Come on and serve," Wally said.

As George prepared to serve, Dick said, "Because she can get good bargains in the summer. Prices always go up before Christmas."

George served into the net, and Wally laughed. "Your turn to get distracted." Wally said.

George felt embarrassment because he had raised an issue about the difficult financial status of Dick and Wally and their mother. He knew their father was dead, and that their mother kept their home going on a limited income. But he didn't know what to say to excuse himself or relieve his embarrassment. He served into the net again, and Wally laughed. They had some more Pepsi, Jerry came back, and soon it was midnight. Back upstairs, Dick checked the clock on the wall.

"Okay," he said. "Time to go. You're going to discover our special process. Let's get our coats on."

So the four boys slipped into their plaid mackinaws, which were the uniform of the time, pulled on knitted hats and gloves, and stepped out into the cold of after-midnight Christmas morning. A slight film of snow had collected and small flakes were drifting down. The boys stood on the porch and considered the snow.

"I didn't bring my overshoes," George said.

"Me neither," Jerry agreed.

Dick looked out into the night. "Well, we better go now before it gets any deeper." He stepped off the porch and the others followed.

"How far do we have to go?" George asked, his words coming out in puffs of steam in the icy night.

"Just to the shopping center," Wally said.

So they walked on, their shoulders hunched against the cold, their gloved hands in their pockets, their heads bent against the chilled wind. They walked through patches of street lights and patches of dark, the fine flakes of snow swirling past them.

When they reached the neighborhood shopping center, lights were still on in the parking lot, but all the stores were dark. There were no cars in the parking lot, and no people in sight.

At one side of the blacktop parking area, a temporary wire fence enclosure had been constructed. On a post above it was a sign, which said in hand-painted letters, "Xmas Trees."

Dick and Wally headed toward the sign, and George and Jerry followed. George looked around. "There's nobody here."

Dick looked back at him and smiled. "That's the idea, bright guy! There's nobody here, they've left for the night. They won't be back tomorrow."

Wally turned and smiled at George and Jerry. "The Christmas tree season is over."

Jerry looked blank. "So?"

Dick and Wally laughed. "So any trees that they left are just going to be thrown out the day after Christmas. They stop selling them at midnight and go home. So we get our choice, and they're free!"

George was still not convinced. "Will there be any left?"

Dick said, nearing the entrance to the fence, "Sure. We do this every year. They never sell them all."

Jerry said, "But they must sell all the good ones." Instantly he felt that he may have said something that would hurt the brothers' feelings. He tried to make amends by adding, "Do you usually find good ones?"

Now they were in the enclosure, and, sure enough, there were several trees left lying about in the snowy darkness. Dick and Wally began to pick them up and stand them at arms length.

"Well," Dick said. "See, guys, it's just a matter of evaluation. You got to look at it and see if it's tall enough or too tall and see if it's bushy enough or not bushy enough, just like you do any other time before tonight." He dropped the one he was holding and stooped to pick up another.

"This one ain't bad," Wally said, slowly turning the one he was holding. The other boys looked at it.

"You're right, Wally," Dick said. "That one ain't bad. It's got one kind of empty spot in it. So we can take another one and cut a couple branches off and tie it in and it will be just about perfect."

Wally looked at George and Jerry. "Hey. So it wasn't a bad idea for you guys to come. So now Dick and I can take a tree by the top and bottom, and you can take a tree by the top and bottom and when we get home we can merge them into one good tree."

Dick laughed. "Not bad for a free tree, huh?"

George and Jerry helped them find a backup tree for the additional limbs they would want, and as quickly as possible they began to carry their trees away through the biting snowy cold.

As they walked, George holding the trunk end of the back up tree, he thought, "Whoever knows what other people do. My dad thinks nothing of paying several dollars for a tree."

They trudged on, and aloud George said, "I bet we end up with a better looking tree then anybody's. You guys are sure smart."

And as they moved from a patch of snowy street lighted sidewalk into the adjoining patch of snowy darkness, George felt a surge of what he interpreted as Christmas spirit rising within him. Somehow he felt unusually good.

He turned his head to look at Wally, who was carrying the tip end of the tree. He couldn't see Wally's face in the darkness, so he turned back to look ahead. But he thought to himself, "I bet Wally feels good too."

Up ahead, through the swirling snow, they could see the light on the porch of Dick and Wally's home.

Chickie's Gift

"We have several cats to give away," my friend from a neighboring town told me on the phone. "Our cat had kittens and the kittens are three months old already and we just can't keep them all around the house. Please say you'll take one."

I laughed. "I wonder what my husband will think?" After a two second pause, "For that matter, I wonder what our landlord will think?" Then I told her, "Let me call you back. The landlord could be dealt with if we were careful with kitty litter and kept the cat indoors."

My husband, after an initial strange look crossed his face, said, "If Chickie likes it, then it's fine with me."

Chickie was our three-year old daughter.

It was mid-December. I said to Rick, my husband, "Let's ask her to hold the kitty until just before Christmas. We'll see if we can't package it up and put it under the tree for Chickie."

My husband smiled, his eyes sparkling. "That'll be something to watch."

Christmas Eve finally came, the tree long since decorated, and we were finally able to get a very excited little girl to bed. Now it was time for Rick to drive across town for the kitten.

We had found a picnic basket, small, wicker, with lots of openings in the wicker for air to pass through. We wrapped it loosely with Christmas paper, leaving openings in the ends for ventilation. We left the cat in its carrier in the garage, not wanting to put it in the basket until Christmas morning.

There were lots of other presents for Chickie. We liked for her to have things that pleased her, and we didn't stint on number or variety. They were all wrapped and under the tree by midnight, and we went to bed, with the alarm set for 4:00. I set it on low, and placed it by my ear so I could hurry to the basement.

When the buzzer sounded at 4:00, I could hardly open my eyes. Rick, bless his heart, sat up and said, "I'll get it. You relax." And he did.

When the dim gray of dawn began peeping through the window, I heard Chickie knocking at our door. Jumping up and grabbing a robe, I opened the door and looked at her bright little eyes. She was in her pajamas, complete with feet. "Are we

206

ready to go down to the tree?" she asked in a voice filled with expectation and awe.

"Ready as soon as your daddy gets up, sweetheart," I laughed.

Rick was getting up, the excitement having communicated itself to him. I saw him struggling into his robe and slippers, and we started down the stairs.

The tree lights were twinkling, dim shafts of early dawn light were filtering through the shades, and the brightly wrapped gifts sparkling in the flashing tree light glow brought a cry of joy from our little Chickie.

"Which would you like to open first?" I asked.

Chickie spread her little hands. "They all look wonderful. Maybe I'll start on this side."

The side she started on included several small packages and the loosely wrapped picnic basket. Because the picnic basket attracted her eyes, she pushed the small gifts aside and grasped the paper covering the basket.

Slowly she peeled the tape aside and pulled the paper off. "It's a picnic basket," she said. "Won't that be fun!"

Rick smiled. "Look inside, Chickie. See if there's something in there."

With hesitant little fingers, Chickie lifted one of the flaps. The kitten stuck its white head through the opening and said a faint meow.

Chickie squealed in delight. Lifting the kitten carefully from the opening, she hugged it to her body and stroked its head. The cat meowed lightly again then began to purr.

"Oh mommy, oh daddy. This is the most wonderful thing I've ever had! Thank you, thank you, thank you!"

In other packages under the tree, there were games played with spinners, games played with play money, rubber horseshoes to be played outdoors, various items of clothing, candies and nuts, a tricycle - all still to be discovered. And an hour later, still holding the kitten, still petting it, still trying out names for it, Chickie finally said, "Mommy, maybe you'll hold Whitey or Snowball or Mittmar, whatever I decide. I think I'll try a few of the other packages."

We never regretted our decision to take the kitten. It was a Christmas morning we'd remember forever.

Christmas In The Country

Eddie jumped out of bed onto the cold floor as weak beams of sunlight filtered through the crack at the bottom of the windowshade. It was Christmas morning, and, peeping through the opening below the shade, he saw heavy white frost on the lawn.

He found his robe at the foot of the bed and hurriedly pulled it around him. It took a little longer to find slippers among the jumble of toys beside the bed, but at last he pulled them onto his feet and hurried out to the hallway, heading past his parents' room and toward the stairway.

"Eddie!" His mother called him as he passed her bedroom door. "This is mighty early for a seven-year-old to be up!"

"Going down to see the presents, mom."

"Do you have your slippers on?"

"Yes, mom. You want to come down now?"

His mother sat up in the bed. Beside her, his father seemed to still be asleep. "We'll go look at them, son. I'm not sure you want to open them before we go to grandma's."

Eddie fidgeted outside her door. "Gosh, mom. If I don't, we go to grandma's and open all the presents out there and eat dinner and then come back it'll be afternoon and I won't have looked at them yet."

His mother came to the door in her slippers and robe. "Well, maybe the thing to do is pick just a few to open now, and save some for when we come back." She looked back at her husband. "Ralph," she said in a louder voice, "you may as well get up. Eddie's raring to go. Come on down in a minute."

"Yeh, dad!" Eddie called to the prone figure beneath the blankets. "Let's get jumping here! It's Christmas morning and there's frost on the ground."

Preceding his mother down the stairs, Eddie hurried to the living room and the pine tree glistening with tinsel and various colors of glass balls. Beneath the tree, colorful even in the dim light, were a number of packages of various shapes and sizes, all wrapped in Christmas paper.

"Wow, mom!" Eddie called back to his mother who had just reached the foot of the stairs. "Sure looks like some good stuff here!"

His mother laughed in response to his enthusiasm. "Well, why don't you pick out two or three that have your name on them. But don't open them until your dad gets here. He'll be down in a minute."

Eddie knelt among the packages, reading labels, shaking some, occasionally laying one aside. "This sounds like something good, mom," he said of one long flat package. "I know it's not socks."

His mother laughed again, as his father joined them and sat in his easy chair. "Okay, go ahead, son. Your dad and I will watch."

"I'll start with these three," Eddie said, pointing to the ones he had laid aside.

"You'll open those three and then we'll get dressed and go to grandma's," his dad said firmly. "We really shouldn't be opening them at all until we come back from grandma's, but your mom is being good to you. So let's see what you've got in those three, son."

Eddie tore into the tissue wrappings and revealed the contents of his three selections. One was a baseball glove.

"Wow, dad! That one was from you. Thanks a lot!"

Another was a large book of stiff cardboard pages, from which parts could be punched out to construct a farm - barns, fences, farmhouse, well, sheds, etc.

"Ain't that neat! And it's from Santa." Eddie looked upward. "Thanks, Santa!"

And the third was a parcheesi game. "This one's from mom. Thanks, mom! I hope you know how to play parcheesi, so you can teach me!"

His mother and dad sat smiling at him for a moment, then his mom stood, saying "All right. That was nice. Your dad and I will save ours until later, because we have to get to grandma's. Hurry and get into your clothes, Eddie. We'll have breakfast when we get there."

The ride to grandma's took them through fields sparkling with the whiteness of the frost. Grandma and Grandpa lived in the country a few miles from town, and it was a family tradition to have as many of the relatives as could make it to gather on Christmas morning for breakfast, then sit around the living room in a large circle, exchanging gifts, opening and displaying them for everyone to see. Each person would open a gift and display it, then wait until everyone else had a turn before the circle was completed, and the person who had opened the first gift would then open his or her next one to display.

The room was filled with aunts, uncles and cousins, as well as Eddie's grandmother, grandfather and his father and mother. He sat on the carpet and squirmed in impatience for his first gift to arrive as it was passed around from hand to hand. Once it was there, he was equally impatient for his turn to open it.

Eventually he had several gifts in bright wrapping paper lying by his feet, and at long last it was his turn to open one. He chose an oblong box and ripped off the paper.

When he lifted the lid, several pairs of multi-colored socks met his eye. His disappointment at not receiving something more appealing to a boy of seven was acute. "Old socks!" he said. There was a slight sneer in his voice.

This reaction was met with a few small nervous laughs around the room. Eddie dropped the box of socks beside him and eagerly fingered another parcel, impatient for his next turn.

Eddie's mother said, from across the room, "Oh Eddie! Those look like wonderful socks. You should thank your grandmother for thinking about keeping your feet nice and warm."

Eddie raised his eyes, turning them to where his grandmother sat. In a flat, small voice, he said, "Thanks grandma."

His grandmother made a small smile and nodded her head. Another package was being opened by one of Eddie's cousins as Eddie felt a finger tap him on the shoulder. He looked up to see his father motioning him toward the door.

"Can you come outside with me a minute, Eddie?" His father was whispering. Whispering in return Eddie said, "I want to see the other packages opened, dad." His father shook his head, frowning. "I need to talk to you for a minute now, Eddie. Now."

Eddie reluctantly rose from his spot in the circle, and moved with his dad toward the door which led to the porch. When they were on the porch, his dad closed the door. Instantly, Eddie was chilled by the frosty morning.

"It's cold out here dad! What did you want?"

His father looked at him sadly. "You've hurt your grandmother's feelings, Eddie. She loves you and thinks of your welfare, and socks are a good thing to get at Christmas. You acted like you didn't like them, and you made her feel bad."

Eddie felt instant regret. "Gosh, I didn't meant to hurt grandma. I'd just rather get something else than socks."

His father shook his head. "Any gift that you get should be appreciated, son. I know you want to see the other people's gifts get open, so let's go back inside. Try to be on your good behavior."

Eddie smiled weakly. "Okay, dad."

Back inside and resuming his spot in the circle, Eddie watched other gifts being opened around the room until finally it was his turn again. This time, the package he opened contained a plaid shirt. It was from one of his aunts. Eddie looked up to find the eyes of the shirt giver.

"Thanks Aunt Susan. That's a nice shirt."

Again the package-opening ceremony circled the room, and Eddie opened additional packages. One was a game, one a book, one was pajamas. Each time, Eddie dutifully raised his eyes to the giver and expressed his thanks, even if sometimes in a mild and subdued voice.

When it was Eddie's turn again, he chose a long flat package and eagerly tore off the wrapping paper. As the gift beneath the wrappings was revealed, Eddie's eyes studied it. It was a book of heavy cardboard pages from which parts could be punched out to build a farm - barn, fencing, shed, farmhouse, etc.

His eyes raised to find the giver of this gift. "It's a book you can make a farm out of. Thanks, Uncle Jack! That's really neat." He showed the gift to the others, smiling.

In two more rounds, the gift-opening ceremony was over. Eddie had also received a sack of marbles and some underwear. Others began to collect their wrapping paper and to move their gifts into neat stacks. Imitating them, Eddie stacked his gifts as well.

"Well, now," Eddie's grandpa said. "I guess it's time for the women folk to start working on the big dinner. I reckon some of the rest of us can listen to the radio. Kids that want to go out and play better get their sweaters."

People rose from around the room. Mothers and aunts heading toward the kitchen, uncles and fathers moved toward grandpa. Kids jumped up and looked for sweaters.

Eddie felt another tap on his shoulder, and knew it was his father. Looking up he said in a whisper, "What now, dad?"

His dad nodded toward the door. "I need to see you for a minute before you start to play."

Eddie's mind raced, trying to think what he might have done. A small lump of anxiety centered in his stomach as he rose to follow his father to the porch.

They stood, momentarily alone. Again the frosty morning bit into Eddie's skin. "What, dad?"

His dad smiled. "I tell you when you do something that isn't too good. That's my duty as your father. But I also tell you when you do something good. I like to be able to tell you when it's something good."

A tentative smile touched Eddie's lips. "I did something good?"

His dad nodded. "When you got that farm book, it was just like the one you have at home. I was afraid you'd say so and Uncle Jack would be upset because he gave you something you already had. It was good of you just to thank him and not tell him that."

Eddie laughed. "Well gee! Thanks, dad. I'm glad that was the right thing to do."

As they started back to the door, Eddie said, "But, see, dad. Having two of them is better than one. You can make twice as big a farm!" He looked up at his father. "Don't you see that, dad? Twice as big a farm!"

Printed in Great Britain
by Amazon